Step

UP

Step UP

ESSENCE BESTSELLING AUTHOR

Monica McKayhan

Recycling programs
for this product may
not exist in your area.

STEP UP

ISBN-13: 978-0-373-83147-0

© 2010 by Monica McKayhan

All rights reserved. The reproduction, transmission or utilization of this work in whole or in part in any form by any electronic, mechanical or other means, now known or hereafter invented, including xerography, photocopying and recording, or in any information storage or retrieval system, is forbidden without written permission. For permission please contact Kimani Press, Editorial Office, 233 Broadway, New York, NY 10279 U.S.A.

This book is a work of fiction. The names, characters, incidents and places are the products of the author's imagination, and are not to be construed as real. While the author was inspired in part by actual events, none of the characters in the book is based on an actual person. Any resemblance to persons living or dead is entirely coincidental and unintentional.

® and TM are trademarks owned and used by the trademark owner and/or its licensee. Trademarks indicated with ® are registered in the United States Patent and Trademark Office, the Canadian Trade Marks Office and/or other countries.

www.KimaniTRU.com

Printed in U.S.A.

For my Granny, Rosa A. Heggie (November 1927–July 2008).
She was special in so many ways, and the strongest woman I knew.
My life is rich because of her.

Acknowledgments

God is the source of my talent and blessings.

For all the young men and women who have enjoyed the Indigo Summer series. Thank you for reading—it's so important! To the parents of my readers, thanks for the encouragement and support. To my family and close friends who keep me grounded—thank you for having my back.

I love you, Evette and Glenda, my editors.
It's been a great ride together.

one

Tameka

BROWN fingertips raced across my swollen belly as raindrops made a pitter-patter sound on the windowpane. It was the first rain in weeks, and I was grateful for it. Atlanta's heat in the summer made the days miserable and the nights were even worse. And being pregnant didn't make things any better. However, Vance had been my knight in shining armor. He'd been by my side from the very beginning—going along for my prenatal appointments, stopping by Publix to pick up whatever strange food I was craving at the moment and taking me for long walks at night just to keep my ankles from swelling. So far he'd kept his promise.

He'd promised that I wouldn't have to do this alone—this teen pregnancy thing. After all, it was both our responsibility, even though he was in denial in the beginning. At first, he questioned whether or not he was actually the father. Then, he all but insisted that I abort the baby—he had hopes and dreams and a scholarship to play ball in college. He thought we were too young to be parents and that a baby would destroy our future. His parents weren't too happy about the idea, either. Vance's dad, Dr. Armstrong, was ready to write me a check and drive me straight to the abortion clinic. They didn't understand that abortion had never been an option for me. My plan was to have this baby regardless of what anybody else wanted. It was my choice, and I had chosen life.

In a few days, Vance would be headed for college. He'd received a full basketball scholarship and classes would be starting soon. Soon, he'd be loading his belongings into the backseat of his car and driving the five hundred miles to Grambling, Louisiana. His best friend Jaylen would be tagging along to college. Jaylen wasn't fortunate enough to receive a scholarship but he was going anyway. The two of them were going to be roommates, despite everyone's advice that they shouldn't share a room. Becoming roommates would destroy their friendship. Everyone could see that. But that was something that they would have to learn the hard way.

As for me, the fall semester would be awkward—wobbling through the halls of our high school would be embarrassing. I would be a spectacle for my friends, teachers and those who were just plain nosy. I dreaded the upcoming school year; got depressed every time I thought about it. It wouldn't be anything nice. The hardest part was quitting the dance team—it was as if someone had stomped on my dreams, picked them up and then stomped on them again.

I wouldn't give up, though. The plan was still to finish high school and graduate as planned. And I was still going to college. Spelman was just around the corner, so I could still go there. I'd work a part-time job and everything would be fine. No worries.

Who was I kidding? I had become a worrier. I woke up every morning with tons of things on my mind—weighing me down like a ton of bricks. So many questions—so many *what-ifs*. What if this pregnancy was too hard for me to handle—what if I got sick or the baby got sick? What if my grades dropped because I was too busy taking care of the baby? What if Vance got to Grambling and met someone new? What if he forgot about the baby and me? So many questions, but the answers weren't so clear.

Vance, on the other hand, didn't have such worries. No one would even know that he had a baby on the way. He could still live in his cozy little world without worries—nothing would really change for him. He'd still play basketball—still chase his dreams. His grades wouldn't suffer because of the baby. He didn't even have to get a part-time job because his parents had already agreed to support the baby and me financially while he was in school. All he had to do was make good grades and play ball.

"This is just as much my responsibility as it is yours," he said. "You're not alone, Tameka, I promise. You and the baby can count on me."

Those were his words, as he stroked my swollen belly. I just hoped that he was for real.

"Did you see that?" I asked, grinning as I stuffed a spoon filled with chocolate ice cream into my mouth.

As the baby kicked his tiny feet underneath my brown skin for the first time, Vance watched with amazement.

"Yeah, I saw it." Vance smiled. "Did that hurt?"

"No, it just feels funny," I said.

"That's so amazing." His eyes were as wide as saucers. "He's really alive in there."

"He?" I asked, with attitude. "Don't you mean *she*?"

"*She* can't play ball."

"*She* can do anything she wants to do. Don't be limiting her," I told him.

"So it's a girl?" he asked. "You cheated, didn't you?"

We had decided to keep the sex of the baby a mystery. I didn't want to know until the baby was born. But the truth was I *had* cheated. I'd waited until Vance left the room during one of our prenatal visits and begged the doctor to spill the beans. Once he told me that my baby was a girl, I never shared the news with Vance. If he knew, he might not have been so excited. When he talked about having a son there was a gleam in his eye that I couldn't risk losing. There was a chance that he might lose interest if he knew it was a girl. And we couldn't afford that. Not right now. Not ever.

"I didn't cheat!" I lied. "We'll both find out when the baby's born."

"Cool." He rested his head on my stomach. "Whatever the baby is—a girl or a boy—I'll be fine with it."

"You serious, Vance?"

"Yeah."

"I can't wait until the three of us can be a family," I said, my eyes becoming dreamy as I stared into Vance's light brown ones.

"Don't get sidetracked, though," he reminded me— snapped me back into reality. "I have seven years of school, and depending on what you decide to major in, you might have just as many. So it'll be a while before we can think about being a family."

"I don't care how long it takes, Vance. It's what I want."

"Don't get all serious on me, Tameka. We're still young, and we still have our whole lives ahead of us. Let's just take it one step at a time. Get through this pregnancy—get through college. That's the most important thing."

He couldn't stop me from dreaming. I couldn't help hoping for the day that the three of us would be together—Vance, me and our baby girl. Lately, it had become my reason—the one thing that kept me going, even when I wanted to give up.

"I know that school's important," I told Vance, "but so is the baby."

"I know the baby's important, Tameka, and I'm here for you. But we gotta stay focused on our goals. And right now, mine is to play ball in college. That's all I'm sayin'.'"

"Cool, Vance." I nudged for him to remove his head from my lap. I was becoming irritated and needed some air. "Let me up."

He sat up and I stood. Wobbled my way through the kitchen and to the back patio. Whenever he avoided the conversation about our future, I pouted. As a matter of fact, I pouted about a lot of things. Pregnancy was like having PMS every day of my life. One minute I'd be laughing and then in the next minute I'd be on the verge of tears. It was a constant roller coaster of emotions, and I was ready to get off the ride.

I plopped down onto a lawn chair.

"I'm sorry, Tameka," Vance said, and then sat in the chair next to mine. He grabbed my hand in his. "I'm here for you. But I wanna take it one step at a time."

"I'm not trippin'," I lied. I *was* trippin'. That's what I seemed to do on a regular basis.

"I gotta get home. Gotta finish packing." Vance pressed his lips against my rosy cheek. "I'll call you later."

I stretched my legs out, checked out my swollen feet. The straps from my flip-flops rested between my toes as I looked at the polish on my toenails. They needed to be redone.

I heard the sliding glass door shut and knew that Vance was really gone. I missed him already, but not nearly as much as I would miss him when he was gone for good. Five hundred miles would be too many miles in between us. Too many miles for him to hold me in his arms when I felt scared. Too many miles for him to feel the kick from his daughter's feet. Too many miles…too many miles…too many miles!

two

Vance

AS the sounds of Tyga bounced through my speakers, I loaded the trunk of my car with plastic containers filled with clothes, my Timberland boots and every pair of Jordans I owned. A box filled with CDs and DVDs, sheets, comforters and a small refrigerator fit perfectly onto the backseat. Jaylen hopped into the passenger seat, let the window all the way down and then adjusted the volume on my stereo. I was happy that he'd chosen to attend Grambling, too. We'd been together since elementary school and there was no need in separating now. He was family, and it would be great to have him around for the next four years. Besides, he needed me. Jaylen struggled in school and I'd always been the one to help him maintain passing grades. Without me, college for him would be a train wreck. And he didn't need that.

Choosing Grambling had been an ordeal, in and of itself. I'd had my eye on Grambling State, and they had their eye on me, too. But it was my father who had insisted on Duke. He wanted nothing more than to see his son attend his alma mater and carry on his legacy. It was no doubt that Duke was a better school all around for sports and academics, but Grambling seemed like it would offer more socially. And if you have to spend four years of your life somewhere, you might as well have fun doing it. It was my mother who convinced me that with a baby on the way, fun was no longer my priority. She argued that I should choose the school that offered me a better future as well as someplace where I would be happy. I decided that *happiness* was the key word, and I would definitely be unhappy at Duke.

My father also wanted me to go to medical school and become a dentist, like him. And for that career, Duke on a full scholarship was the right choice. Not to mention Duke had always been a top ten basketball school and I definitely wanted to be where the winners were. But I wasn't interested in med school—not even a little bit. Since I was a little kid, my mother's career as a lawyer had always sparked my interest. It was law school that I was most interested in. I was definitely not interested in pulling anybody's rotten teeth for a living. I had plans of following in my mother's footsteps and was headed for law school. Dad wasn't happy about my college choice, but eventually he started speaking to me again.

As I stood next to my car, the Atlanta heat beaming against my face, I wondered what the next few years would be like. Mom ran out of the house carrying a plastic Wal-Mart bag, and Dad was behind her carrying a red-and-white cooler.

"We packed you some things for the ride," Mom said and handed me the bag. It was filled with sandwiches, snack cakes and fresh fruit.

"Some Cokes and bottled water." Dad held the cooler into the air and then looked for a spot on the backseat for it.

"Thanks," I said and wanted to keep the conversation light. Mom was on the verge of tears, and she'd already cried twice.

"You call us every hour and check in," she said. "Is your phone charged?"

"To capacity," I told her. I'd made sure it had a full charge before I loaded my things into the car. "Plus I got my car charger just in case. And if mine goes dead, Jaylen's got his phone, too."

"And you got a full tank of gas?"

"Yes, Ma. You're worrying again," I told her.

"Sweetheart, the boy will be fine," Dad interjected and then wrapped his arm around Mom. "Ease up a little."

"He's my baby! I can't ease up." She pushed him away. "And he's going away…for real. Not just for a weekend, but for real."

"Christmas will be here before you know it," Dad said, "and he'll be home."

"Okay y'all," I interrupted, "I wanna go ahead and get on the road. I want it to be daylight when we make it on campus. You know, so we can check things out a little bit."

"Be careful on that road, Vance," Mom said and then grabbed me; hugged me tightly. "Do the speed limit…you know the highway patrol don't play."

"I know, Ma." I kissed her forehead.

"Love you, sweetie," she said and caressed my face, tears in her eyes. "You, too, Jaylen." Mom leaned her head into the car's window. "Did you tell your mama goodbye?"

That was a stupid question. Did she think he just ran out of the house and didn't say anything to his parents?

"Yes, ma'am, I did." He smiled at my mother. "She cried, too, Mrs. A."

"Let me give the boy a hug so he can go," Dad said and pulled me into an embrace. "Love you, son."

"Love you, too, Dad."

"Take care, Jaylen," Dad said.

"You, too, Dr. A," Jaylen said.

"Goodbye, stupid!" Lori yelled from the porch. "I get your room now!"

"In your dreams," I told my little sister.

"I'll be moving my things in as soon as you pull off." She grinned.

"You better not go anywhere near my room, and I'm so serious." I gave her a mean mug. "Ma, please don't let her go in my room."

"She's just messing with you, baby," Mom said.

"Get over here and give me a hug with your big head," I said to my sister.

"Ewww! No," she said and then flipped open her pink phone; pretended to be calling someone.

I rushed toward her anyway, picked her up and threw her over my shoulder and twirled her around in the air.

"Let me down, Vance!" she yelled.

"Bye, ugly," I said as I let her down. I messed up her hair before running to my car and hopping into the driver's seat. "You know you're gonna miss me."

"Ooh, I hate you!" she yelled. "Don't ever come back."

"I'll be back for Christmas. Maybe even Thanksgiving." I smiled at my mother and started my car. "I'll call you in a little bit, Mom. Please don't cry. It's not as bad as it seems."

She made it extremely hard for me to pull off, but I had to. I pulled out of the driveway and then headed down our quiet street. Took a glance into the rearview mirror and watched as my parents waved goodbye to me. They acted as if I was moving to a foreign country, shaving my head bald, joining a cult and never returning to the United States. It wasn't that serious.

I took the back roads to Tameka's house. She'd made me promise to stop by for a few minutes. She was outside when

I pulled up, her face glowing in the sunlight and her belly a little round bubble on the front of her body. She wore a pink T-shirt that was much too tight around her stomach, denim shorts and pink flip-flops on her feet. As soon as I hopped out of the car, she was standing by my side.

"What took you so long?" she asked.

"Had to load my car and pry myself away from my parents. Especially my mother," I explained.

"She's just gonna miss you, Vance. And so am I."

"Gonna miss you, too." I kissed the tip of her nose. "But if me and Jaylen don't get on the road soon, it'll be dark when we get there."

I had already said my goodbyes to Tameka the night before, holding her while tears filled her eyes. She had so many fears about my leaving, and so many questions. She was concerned that I might meet someone new, or that I might forget about her. She wanted to know how much partying I planned on doing and if I would still call and send text messages on a regular basis.

"I just wanted to see your face again...before you left." She smiled. "You look fly in your Celtics jersey, with your fresh haircut. You smell good, too."

I had chosen my Kevin Garnett jersey and my Calvin Klein cologne for the drive. Not that anybody would be smelling my cologne except Jaylen. It would be worn off by the time we got to Grambling, but I didn't care. I would just refresh it once I got there.

"I'll see you, girl. You take care of my baby. And call me as soon as you start having pains or if your water breaks. I don't know if I'll be able to come home, but I'll sure try."

"I'm glad you're still going away to college, Vance. I'm glad the baby didn't ruin it for you."

"You can still go, too, Tameka. The baby doesn't have to ruin it for anyone. It'll be hard, but you can do it. I believe in you."

"I believe in you, too, Vancey Pants."

She'd come up with this new nickname for me and it drove me crazy...sounded feminine...*Vancey Pants*.

"I don't know about that name," I said. "It sounds kind of sissified."

"You're just being homophobic." She laughed and then wrapped her arms around me, her stomach in between us. Her lips found mine and we kissed. "I love you."

"Love you, too," I told her.

Love. It was such a strong word. I wasn't quite sure what it meant for us. I only said it because I thought I should; because my baby was growing in her stomach. Because I was leaving and wouldn't be back anytime soon. It seemed the right thing to say, especially since she'd said it to me first. You could love people all day long—heck, I loved Jaylen for that matter. We were brothers, and had been for many years. I guessed I could love Tameka, too.

"Let's go, bro," Jaylen said. "Tell that girl bye and let's go."

"Shut up, Jaylen," Tameka said and stuck her tongue out at him.

"I really do need to go," I told her and pulled myself from her embrace. "I'll call you."

"When?" she asked.

"As soon as I get there," I said and then exhaled when she shook her head okay. I was grateful that she didn't want a phone call every hour like my mother did.

I hopped into my car and started the engine. Tameka stepped back, the palm of her hand caressing her belly. She waved and then blew me a kiss.

I breezed through the streets of College Park and then

hopped onto I-20 headed west. With the wind blowing through the windows, and Tyga rapping in my ears, I knew that Jaylen and I were just a few hours away from being full-fledged college men.

three

Marcus

Harvard. It looked nothing like the pictures I'd seen on the Internet. It was far more interesting, with its old buildings and beautiful green grass. It was fascinating when I found out that Harvard had been around since the pilgrims had landed on Plymouth. I'd read about the pilgrims in elementary school, but to actually see a piece of history in real life was a trip. Harvard started out with nine students, and I tried to imagine how a college with so few people had grown into a university with more than eighteen thousand students trying to get a degree. So much history on these grounds, I thought. One of the buildings called Massachusetts Hall was where the soldiers of the Continental army had stayed during the Revolutionary War.

As I took a look around, I could almost imagine President Barack Obama walking these grounds when he attended Harvard as a law student. In fact, he was the first African American president of the *Harvard Law Review.* The *Harvard Law Review*—a journal written by students at Harvard about important legal issues. No other person of color had been *Law Review* president. The first African American president of the *Harvard Law Review* and the first

African American president of the United States. So many firsts for him. He was someone that I could look up to, be proud of. I took a long, deep breath and then exhaled. Harvard was going to be cool.

After picking up the key to my dorm, I dragged my black suitcase on wheels across the courtyard toward Harvard Square. Wearing a pair of denim shorts, a red T-shirt and Nike flip-flops, I held on to the strap of my gym bag that was heavy on my shoulder. I had intended to pack light, but it was hard considering I had to pack enough for seven weeks. Every pair of Jordans I owned was stuffed inside the gym bag, along with a pair of dress shoes. Pop had insisted on the dress shoes, a pair of slacks and a button-down shirt with a collar.

"You might need to dress up, son. You just never know," he'd said.

He was more excited about the summer at Harvard than I was. Which was amazing because the first time I'd told Pop of my plans for college, he had frowned on them. Said that I needed to stick closer to home and be prepared to take over our family's property management business. But it seemed that the closer I got to my senior year in high school, the easier it was for me to talk to him about college. In fact, when I first mentioned the summer program at Harvard, he encouraged me to apply. And when I told him how much it was going to cost, he didn't even flinch.

"I've been saving my money, and I got part of it," I explained to Pop, "and what I can't cover, I can probably get some financial aid."

I wanted to make sure that Pop knew how important it was to me—so much so that I was willing to pay my own way. Every year, high school students from all over the world spent the summer on Harvard's campus, attending college classes and getting a taste of what it was like to be a college student. I knew that Harvard was my number one college choice, and I couldn't think of a better way of spending my summer or my money, especially since my senior year was fast approaching. In the fall, I would be one of the big dogs at my high school. Preparing for my last year of high school and my future was the most important thing at the moment.

"I've been saving some money, too, Marcus. Started putting it in a trust fund about a year ago, just in case you were really serious about going to this Ivy League school," Pop said. "Ain't that the school Barack Obama went to?"

"Sure is." I smiled.

"Yeah, that's where I want you to go, son. Maybe you'll mess around and become the president of the United States one of these days." Pop laughed. "How much money you say you need for that summer program?"

Pop had written a check for the full balance to pay for my summer classes, room and board. I made sure my application was one of the first ones they received, especially since early applications received priority. Unfortunately, some people ended up on a waiting list and I was determined that it wouldn't be me. I had received my acceptance letter two weeks after I'd submitted it. I didn't waste any time registering for my classes.

I stuck my key into the lock and entered my dorm suite, dropped my gym bag onto the floor before pulling my suitcase into the room. My roommate had already claimed the bed closest to the window; his garment bag sprawled across the twin bed and there was a pair of tan loafers on the floor beneath the bed. A laptop computer sat on top of the desk across the room, its battery being charged in one of the electrical outlets on the wall. I claimed the empty bed and dropped my bags next to it.

I sat on the edge of the bed and flipped open my cell phone. Indigo had called twice and left three text messages since I'd left Atlanta early that morning. She'd tagged along to the airport with my father when he dropped me off at the curb. Tears had filled her eyes as we hugged and said our goodbyes. She acted as if seven weeks would be a lifetime, when it wasn't the first time that we'd been apart for the summer. The summer before, Indigo had spent the entire time in Chicago with her Nana Summer and I had spent my vacation in Houston with my mom. We'd made a pact to break up and then get back together at the end of the summer, provided neither of us met someone new. That was a year ago, and we both agreed that it was a stupid pact and that we should never have agreed to it. But this was different. This wasn't really a vacation; this was my future. And I had no intentions of meeting anyone new. Indigo was my girl for life.

I checked my text messages.

Safe travels. That was the first one.

U there yet? That was the second text message.

Miss u already…can u call me?

I hadn't had time to miss Indigo. From the moment I rushed through the automatic doors at Hartsfield-Jackson Airport, I had made a mad dash for the ticket counter to get my boarding pass and then rushed through the security checkpoint. I had just enough time to grab a sausage, egg and cheese biscuit at Burger King before I reached my gate. Agents were already boarding my flight by the time I got there. Once on board, I reclined in my seat. Headphones on my ears, I flipped through a *Sports Illustrated* magazine. I'd already started to doze before thoughts of Indigo had time to enter my head.

Once I'd reached Logan Airport in Boston, I hit the ground

running. I purchased a CharlieTicket for two dollars at the train station and hopped on the "T" and headed for South Station where I would transfer to the Red Line subway that would take me to Harvard Square. I had enough on my mind just trying to get from the airport to campus. I had caught the MARTA train in Atlanta a million times, but this new subway system in a new city meant that getting around would be a challenge for me. Exiting the "T" at Harvard Yard, I'd been on a mission. No time for phone calls or text messages.

Made it safely. I sent a text to Indigo and then dialed my father's number. He didn't pick up, so I left him a voice message that my flight had landed and I was already on campus. I slipped my shoes from my feet, leaned back onto my bed. Before long, I was fast asleep.

The sound of laughter and voices shook me from my nap. I checked my face for drool and sat straight up.

"You Marcus?" An Asian-looking boy wearing khaki shorts, a white polo shirt and leather sandals stood in front of me. His shiny black hair was combed to the back of his head. He held his hand out to me.

"Yes, I am," I said and grabbed his hand in a firm handshake.

"I'm Jae-Hwa," he said. "Just call me Jae."

Jae's English was broken and he looked as if he struggled to get it right.

"You're an international student?" I asked.

"From Korea," said Jae. "And you?"

"I'm from Atlanta," I told Jae.

"Atlanta?" he asked. Puzzled, he frowned.

"Atlanta, Georgia," I said. "You heard of it?"

"I heard of the state of Georgia. Yes. It's here…in the United States." He grinned, as if he'd made a sudden discovery.

"I bet it took you forever to get here from Korea!" I exclaimed. "How long did it take?"

"Take?" he asked.

"Yeah, how long? You know…on the airplane…" I moved my hand in the air as if it were an airplane moving across the sky.

"Oh, airplane." Jae smiled. "Long time to fly on airplane. Twenty-eight hours."

"It took you twenty-eight hours to fly here, man?" I thought I'd heard him wrong. That seemed like an extremely long time to be on a plane, especially since my two-hour flight from Atlanta had me restless. I couldn't imagine flying for twenty-six hours longer.

"Yes. Long time." Jae smiled again. "You hungry, Marcus?"

"Yeah, I could eat." I rubbed my stomach.

"You would like to go eat?" Jae asked. "Dinner in ten minutes. We could go together."

"Yeah, that'll be cool," I said and stood. Slipped my flip-flops back on my feet.

"Cool?" Jae asked, that puzzled look on his face again.

Realizing he wasn't familiar with my slang, I said, "Dinner would be nice, Jae. Let's go eat."

Annenberg Hall was impressive with its grand ceiling, hanging chandeliers and stained glass windows like the ones you would find in a Catholic church. With wooden tables and chairs in perfect rows along the shiny wood floors, the dining hall was filled with laughter and loud conversations. Jae and I found a couple of empty seats next to two white guys and a short black guy who needed a haircut—like yesterday.

"Hey." The first white guy stretched his hand my way and in his British-sounding accent he said, "I'm Paul. Paul Chapman."

I took his hand in a firm handshake. "I'm Marcus Carter. And this here's Jae-Hwa."

"This is Chris Matthews and Derrick Smith." Paul introduced his friends. "I believe we're all roommates at Claverly Hall."

"No kidding," I said, taking a long hard look at the guys who I'd be living with for the next seven weeks.

Jae and I shook hands with everyone.

"Where're you from, Marcus?" Paul asked.

"Atlanta," I said. "And you?"

"London," Paul said.

"I'm from Yellowknife," Chris stated.

Jae and I glanced at each other, puzzled.

"It's in Idaho," Chris added and smiled.

"I'm from Alaska," Derrick announced. "I'm a computer geek. I could tap into Fort Knox if I wanted to, which is why my father all but insisted that I join the marines. He's been a marine since before I was born, and I was supposed to become a marine, too. I think I disappointed him when I chose Harvard."

"Yeah, that's like my father," Paul said. "A member of the British armed forces who runs a tight ship. I was supposed to join the British navy but I insisted on college. I'd rather attend UCLA or somewhere warm like Florida. But he insisted that if I must go to college, then Harvard would be my only choice."

"Same here." I added, "I'm supposed to take over our family business rather than go to college at all."

"Where the heck are you from, Jae?" Chris asked. "Japan…China…?"

"I'm from Seoul, Korea," Jae answered, even though he didn't realize he'd just been insulted.

I glanced at Chris, trying to figure him out. I wondered if he was making fun of Jae or if he just lacked manners.

"Korea?" Chris asked. "Why didn't you just do the summer program there? Harvard has this same program in Korea."

"I wanted to come to the States," Jae said.

"That makes sense," Paul said and then quickly changed the subject. He obviously felt the same way about the vibe he got from Chris. "Marcus, what classes are you taking?"

"Applied Mathematics," I said, "and of course African and African American Studies."

"You have to study being an African American?" Chris laughed. "Haven't you been one all your life?"

"Are you taking any history classes, Chris?" I asked.

"Of course." Chris smiled.

"Whose history will you be studying?" I asked.

"Who is this guy?" he asked no one in particular. "American History, of course."

"Haven't you been an American all of your life?" I asked.

Chris gave me a sideward glance before our conversation was interrupted by someone on a microphone.

"May I have your attention, please?" the female voice asked, "Attention, please…everyone…"

Voices were silenced throughout the room.

"I would like to welcome each of you to Harvard University. We know that this is an exciting and wonderful time for each of you…."

While I listened to the speech, I glanced over at Chris. He was different. But so were all of us. All the faces sprinkled around the room, each was different one from the other—a mixture of white, yellow and brown faces. Everyone was from somewhere else, with a different story. All had different goals and dreams, but one common goal: to make the most of their summer at Harvard. Nothing I had ever done in my life could compare with this—except, of course, making Indigo my girl. And even that was a close second.

four

Tameka

I heard the doorbell but tried to ignore it as I listened to Rocsi from 106 & Park as she introduced the next musical guest.

"You don't hear that doorbell ringing?" Mommy asked as she wiped her hands on a dish towel.

I just gave her a look of unconcern. I knew it was my friends Indigo, Asia, Jade and Tymia on the other side of the door because they'd just sent a text message and said that they were pulling up in front of my house. I wasn't ready to see them, not with a belly the size of a watermelon and swollen feet. They would ask too many questions and stare too hard. They knew I was pregnant, but hadn't seen me since the last day of school. My weight had almost doubled since then. They were my friends, but it was so much easier to alienate myself from everyone.

"It's Indi," Mommy said. "And Asia, Jade...and that other little girl...what's her name?"

"Tymia," I responded but my eyes never left the television set.

"What's the matter, baby?" Mommy asked. "Don't you wanna see your friends?"

"Not really," I said. "Can you just get rid of 'em?"

"No, Tameka. I won't do that. These girls are your friends and they just wanna make sure you're okay."

"They just wanna be all up in my business."

"I refuse to believe that," Mommy whispered. "I'm opening this door."

It was no secret that pregnancy caused you to have mood swings, and most of the time you just wanted to be alone. The summer was hot already, and my body was taking on a mind of its own. My life was different from the lives of my friends. They were still dancers on the hottest dance team in Atlanta. They could still wear sexy jeans from the 5-7-9 store and cute little shirts that were on sale at Charlotte Russe for the summer. They could strut their stuff in bikinis from Victoria's Secret and could slide their feet into a pair of flip-flops from Old Navy without feeling like their toes were going to burst. Their lives had not changed one bit, while mine was suddenly doing somersaults.

Mommy swung the door opened and I couldn't help noticing Indigo's flawless skin. She wore a hot pink tank top and denim shorts, leather flip-flops on her feet. Asia toppled in the door behind her wearing a colorful sundress. Tymia followed with a pair of white capris and a fuchsia-colored top with matching lip gloss. Jade was pulling up the rear in a pair of khaki shorts and a multicolored top with spaghetti straps.

"What's up, girl?" Asia asked.

"Did you get my text?" Indi asked. "I've left you like a hundred text messages."

"Yeah, and I called you twice yesterday," Tymia added.

"Are you avoiding us?" Indigo plopped down on the sofa next to me and snatched the remote from my hand. Jade took a seat next to Indi, and Asia and Tymia both took seats on the love seat across the room.

"I didn't feel like talking," I admitted. No need in sugar-coating the truth.

My hair was all over my head and I still had on pajamas. I had brushed my teeth that morning, but a shower wouldn't have been a bad thing.

"Can I get you girls something to drink?" Mommy asked as she opened the blinds and let sunshine in.

"No, thank you," they all said in unison.

"You should all stay for dinner," Mommy said and smiled at me. "I'm making spaghetti with meatballs."

"Ooh, that sounds good!" Jade exclaimed. "Count me in, Mel."

"Me, too," Indigo said.

"Who's on 106 & Park today?" Asia asked.

"Robin Thicke," I mumbled. "It's a rerun, though."

"Did you really think that you could avoid us, girl-friend?" Indigo asked and started flipping through the channels as if she was at home, and as if I wasn't already watching something.

"I was hoping." I snatched the remote from her and switched the channel back to BET.

"Well, it won't be that easy to get rid of us. We're here to stay," Tymia announced. "Now stand up and let us see how phat you are. And when I say phat, I mean P-H-A-T!"

"You look really cute. And you're glowing," Asia said.

"And your hair is so long and healthy looking." Indigo ran her fingers through my hair. "But you need to do something with these nails. Let me see what I got in my purse to help you out."

Indigo started digging through her purse—for what, I wasn't sure. They acted as if nothing had changed; as if my body wasn't the size of a Goodyear blimp. I had been so scared that their visit would be weird and uncomfortable, and so I had avoided all thoughts of seeing them. But I suddenly found myself glad that they had stopped by. It was as if we hadn't missed a beat—as if we were still the same friends that we'd always been.

"You need a pedicure…like…yesterday." Jade frowned as she glanced at my toes.

"Why don't we all go and get pedicures!" Asia was always so bubbly.

"I'm not leaving this house." I made that clear.

"Ever?" Tymia asked.

"Not until the end of the summer. I can't risk someone from school seeing me." My mind was made up.

"You're joking, right?" Jade asked.

"I'm very serious."

"What about when school starts?" Indigo asked. "Everybody's gonna see you then."

"I'll cross that bridge when I get to it," I said. "Now can we drop it?"

"Cool…it's dropped." Indigo grabbed my hand and began trimming my nails with a fingernail clipper.

As Robin Thicke serenaded us on 106 & Park, I laughed and talked with my friends like old times. Soon after, we ate spaghetti and meatballs at my dining room table and gossiped about everybody we could think of.

"So, have you heard from Vance since he left for Grambling?" Jade asked.

"Shut up!" Indi shushed Jade. "He's only been gone a few days."

"To answer your question…he sent a text when he got there. But I haven't heard from him since…." There was a long silence in the room. It was the first time since they showed up that I felt uncomfortable. I broke the silence. "Indi, I heard that Marcus went away to Harvard for the summer."

"Yep, he left Saturday morning." She pouted. "I miss him already."

"At least he's coming back in a few weeks. Unlike Vance who won't be home until Thanksgiving or Christmas."

Nobody said anything. It was as if they were afraid to touch the subject of Vance being gone.

"Can you pass me the garlic bread?" Tymia asked, and I handed her the glass dish filled with bread.

From that moment on, we kept the conversation light. Being pregnant brought about more challenges than I was ready for.

five

Vance

Basketball camp turned out to be more than I'd bargained for, with its early morning gatherings and exercise that had my body sore in places that I didn't know could ache. High school practices had nothing on this. This was boot camp—with a vengeance. Waking up at four o'clock in the morning during the summer and spending the entire day on the court—that was my day in a nutshell.

The shriek of Coach Lang's whistle sent us sprinting back and forth across the court; our last set of exercises before the day ended, and I was grateful. I could almost taste that Riptide Rush-flavored Gatorade that was waiting for me on the bench next to Jaylen. He was already turning up his own bottle as he waited for me to get done with practice.

After practice, I headed for the locker room, packed my gym bag and headed for the gym again.

"You owe me for this, son. Gatorade ain't cheap," Jaylen said, handing me a towel and my bottle when we were done as we strolled out of the gym.

"Gas ain't cheap either, but I don't see you handing me

any gas money every time you hop into my car," I said and stole a glance at two beautiful girls as they strolled down the sidewalk of our campus.

"Come on, V man. You know I'm just messing with you."

"Yeah, whatever," I said and wiped sweat from my forehead. "Let's grab something to eat. I'm starved."

One of the girls looked my way and smiled. I smiled back as they approached.

"Hey," the caramel-colored girl with long silky hair said. "You Vance Armstrong?"

"Yeah," I said.

"I'm Shay," she said. "I heard you're pretty good on the court."

"I can do a little something-something," I boasted, and rubbed the whiskers underneath my chin.

Shay smiled and then introduced her chocolate-colored friend. "This is Kim."

"How you doing, Kim?" I asked. "This is my boy, Jaylen."

"Are y'all going to the frat party on Friday night?" Kim asked.

I'd heard the buzz about the frat party that everybody who was anybody was attending.

"Of course," I stated matter-of-factly.

"Will you be there?" Jaylen asked Kim.

"I might," Kim said, "but I don't hang out with fresh meat."

"Kim!" Shay exclaimed. "Be nice."

"What?" Kim laughed and then ran her finger behind Jaylen's ear. "Look…he's still wet behind the ears."

"Oh, you got jokes." Jaylen was embarrassed and I was embarrassed for him.

"I'm just messing with you, sweetie." Kim smiled and grabbed Jaylen's chin. "You be a good boy and Kim might show you around a little bit. Okay?"

Jaylen grinned. He was like a little kid at that moment. "Okay," he said.

Jaylen had been punked and now he was acting like one. I wasn't about to give them the satisfaction of making me feel like less of a man.

"I hope to see you there, Vance," Shay cooed, one little cute dimple on the side of her cheek.

"Yeah, I might show up…depending on my schedule," I said, not wanting her to think I was still wet behind my ears, too. I wasn't going out like my man, Jay.

"I'll look for you." Shay's fingertip caressed my face.

I tried not to stare at her ample round behind and she walked away, but I couldn't help sneaking a peek. She was cute but I didn't need any distractions. I had a girl at home who was depending on me to do the right thing. And that's what I intended on doing. I was here to get an education and to play ball.

"She like me," Jaylen said. "She just playing a little hard to get. But I'ma break her down."

"Dude, that girl is not interested in you…not even a little bit."

"Pil-lease! That girl want me so bad," Jaylen announced. "She gon' be mine before the end of the summer. You watch."

Jaylen and I strolled over to the McCall dining hall for a bite to eat. Loud conversations filled the room as we walked in, grabbed a tray and went through the food line. We approached a table in the center of the cafeteria.

"Anybody sittin' here?" I asked the tall brother from the basketball team. We hadn't met yet. There were so many teammates that I didn't know, and all of them were from other parts of the country.

"Nah, man. Have a seat," he said. "I'm Chauncey."

"Vance," I said and grabbed his hand in a firm handshake. "This is my boy, Jaylen."

"You looked pretty good out there on the court today in practice. Where you from, bro?" Chauncey asked.

"Atlanta."

"What brought you to this little country town, man? There are so many good schools in Atlanta."

"Just always wanted to go here. Seemed like a good place to be," I explained.

I wasn't sure when my infatuation with Grambling started, but I knew that I wanted to be at a historically black college, where I could meet some interesting people, get a good education and play some ball.

"I thought about Georgia State myself," Chauncey said. "I hope you brought plenty of mosquitoes repellant. A city boy like yourself won't make it down here in these backwoods."

"Not for long," said another brother from the team as he walked up. He slapped hands with Chauncey. "Where is this city boy from?"

"From the A-T-L," Chauncey announced as if I wasn't sitting there.

"What's he doing down in the country?"

"I don't know, man." Chauncey laughed. "This here's Vance and Jaylen."

"I'm Harlen." Jaylen and I both shook Harlen's hand.

"What fraternity you looking at?" Chauncey asked.

The truth was I hadn't even given it a thought. I didn't know much about fraternities except that they threw good parties. And sometimes they did stuff for the community. I'd also heard about some of the things that people did to join a fraternity—crazy things. The thought of joining a fraternity had never interested me—hadn't even crossed my mind before.

"Um…I hadn't really thought about it," I admitted.

"We're Alphas," Chauncey said, his chest all stuck out. "Alpha Phi Alpha Fraternity."

"I pledged freshman year," Harlen announced.

"When you consider Greek life here on campus, make sure you consider us first," Chauncey said. "An organization of true brotherhood. Alpha Phi Alpha set the standard for other black fraternities...been around for over a hundred years."

"Founded by a group of brothers from Cornell University." Harlen gave us a history lesson. "Dr. Martin Luther King...you know who he was, right?"

Of course we knew Dr. King...was he kidding? What black person on the face of the earth didn't know who Dr. King was? Not to mention, we'd just driven five hundred miles from Atlanta, Georgia, Dr. King's hometown.

"Of course we know who Dr. King was," I said.

"Dr. King was an Alpha," Harlen stated.

"Thurgood Marshall, too," Chauncey added, "and Keenan Ivory Wayans. I know you know him."

"Yeah, I know him," Jaylen said.

"But what do we care?" I asked. "We're just here to play ball, get a good education and party a little bit."

"But what about your future?" Harlen asked. "What about building strong relationships with men who can help you become leaders? Relationships that last a lifetime? Nothing better than that."

"Okay, say we were interested in something like that...what do we have to do?"

"Well, you can't join until you've completed at least one semester of school," Chauncey said.

"And there's a minor initiation period," Harlen added.

"Aw, here we go," Jaylen said.

"What about hazing?" I asked. I'd heard about some members of Greek organizations who had been arrested for taking the initiation process too far.

"Hazing is against the law and something that Alphas have

taken a strong stand against. I promise you will not have to participate in anything life threatening," said Chauncey.

"Give it some thought." Harlen stood, grabbed his tray. "Come and see us when you're potty trained."

Laughter echoed across the cafeteria. Chauncey stood and the two of them headed for the door. Jaylen and I looked at each other and shrugged. We had a lot to learn about campus life.

SIX

Marcus

BY the time I stepped into my physics class, the professor was already lecturing. Embarrassed, I slid into a seat near the back of the room, gently placed my backpack on the floor, loosened its Velcro and pulled my book out. No one seemed to care that I was late, or that I'd gotten lost and ended up outside of Widener Library instead of the building where my class was. They didn't know that I'd just sprinted across campus, dropped my backpack twice and lost a flip-flop before finally stepping into the air-conditioned building. No one looked my way or even asked "are you lost?" And once inside the classroom, only a few eyes watched as I scanned the room for an empty seat. The professor never once stopped talking and wasn't the least bit distracted when I walked in. In high school, the teacher would've stopped in the middle of the lecture and asked me a million questions about why I was late.

"He's on page ninety-six," whispered a cappuccino-colored girl with long silky hair as I slid into the seat next to her. Her smile seemed to make her entire face glow. With teeth that were perfect and white, she was the most beautiful thing I'd seen since I'd left Indigo Summer at the curb at

Hartsfield-Jackson Airport in Atlanta. Besides the African boy at the front of the class and me, she was the only other person of color in the entire room.

"Thanks," I whispered back, and turned to page ninety-six in my textbook.

I opened my spiral notebook to a blank page in order to take notes, and by the time class was over, two pages were completely filled. I'd never taken so many notes. I thought he'd never stop lecturing as I closed my book and stuffed it back into my backpack. The cappuccino-colored girl stood. She wore a denim jacket and khaki shorts against her long shiny brown legs.

As she gathered her books, her light brown eyes looked my way. "You a freshman?"

I wasn't sure how to answer. I wasn't quite a freshman, since I was still technically in high school. But I didn't necessarily want her to know that I was just there for the summer program and that I'd be headed back to my College Park high school in a few weeks; back to being a teenager with a curfew and a part-time job at Wendy's. It would be so much more interesting to make her believe that I was a big-time college student with a college course syllabus stuffed into my backpack and a major that I was actually trying to achieve. I was a Harvard man, after all.

"Something like that," I answered, and then quickly changed the subject. "I'm Marcus."

"Daria," she said and held her hand out to me. I took her small palm into my hand and shook it. "I thought maybe you were here for the summer program."

Busted. Did I have High School Kid plastered across my forehead, or did I look as if I had milk in the corners of my mouth? I guess I didn't fit the profile of the average Harvard student; maybe I didn't have the bags under my eyes from staying up all night studying or I wasn't as refined as some of the college men that she knew. After all, I was from urban Atlanta—right off of Old National Highway, a major road that ran right through the hood. What was a boy from College Park, Georgia, doing on the campus of an Ivy League school right in the middle of Cambridge, Massachusetts?

"I am here for the summer program," I admitted—*reluctantly*. "I'm from College Park, Georgia. What about you?"

"I'm from Riverdale, Georgia." She smiled. "Small world, huh?"

"No doubt." I couldn't help but grin at the fact that Daria was a Georgia peach.

"What time is your next class?" she asked.

"I'm done for the day," I said.

"Me, too. Come on. Let's go grab a bite to eat, Marcus."

"Cool," I said and then swung my backpack on to my shoulder.

Daria and I stepped outside into the afternoon sunshine. Before I knew it we were headed for the "T," Boston's subway station. I dug into my pockets to make sure I had change for the "T," and also enough for a burger or whatever we decided to grab to eat. Pulling two dollars out of my pocket, I stepped in front of the machine in order to buy a CharlieTicket.

I plopped down into an available seat and Daria slid in next to me. It was then that I noticed the smell of her cologne—enticing. I took a glance at her long slender legs; didn't want her to catch me taking a peek so I quickly looked away, but the memory of them stayed stuck in my mind. They were silky smooth. She had a nice set of toes, too—not crusty or funny shaped. I adjusted in my seat, peered out the window as the train came to a halt at Central Square Station.

"This is us," Daria announced and stood.

I stood, too, and then we squeezed through the crowd and onto the platform. I followed her up a flight of stairs and onto the sidewalk. As we stepped into the coffeehouse, the aroma of coffee and pastries hit my nose immediately. Several people lounged in furniture around the room. Students studied for tests or simply read novels in the corners of the room. A few people punched the keys on their laptop computers. One guy, dressed in an old T-shirt and cut-off khaki shorts, sent a text message from his iPhone. Conversations were low as light jazz played. Daria stepped up to the counter as a cheerful girl greeted her with a smile.

"What can I get for you?"

"I'll have the iced latte," Daria said, "and a banana muffin."

"And you, sir?" The girl behind the counter turned to me.

"Um, I'll just have a Coke."

"We don't sell Coke." She gave me a smile; one that said she understood that I was a fish out of water.

Coffeehouses weren't my thing. At home, I hung out at the mall or at the gym at school after practice. My friends and I might end up at McDonald's or Burger King after a game, but never a coffeehouse. The only other time I'd stepped foot into a place like this was the time Pop wanted to see what all the hype of Starbucks was about. He'd dragged me along as he ordered a cappuccino and then complained about how much it costs.

"Hmm," I said, scanning the menu. "I'll just have what she's having."

"So, two iced lattes?" she asked, just to be sure.

"Yeah," I answered, "and that muffin thing, too."

"So two iced lattes and two banana muffins?"

"Yes," Daria said to the girl, and then turned to me. "You don't drink coffee much, huh?"

"Nah. Not that much."

"Marcus, you should get out more." Daria laughed. "This is where most of the kids hang out. People mostly come here to study or to just unwind after class. You'll find yourself here a lot."

"This is how you unwind?" I asked. "What about listening to some R & B on your iPod, or checking out an episode of 106 & Park or something? That's how I unwind."

"Yeah, me, too. When I was in high school," she said. "I don't really have much time for 106 & Park anymore."

After we were handed our drinks, two chairs near the window suddenly became available.

"Let's grab those seats!" Daria said and rushed over and sat down before someone else could claim the vacant seats. "This place gets really crowded and quick."

"So you come here a lot?" I asked, my body sinking into the plush velvet chair.

"Only when I'm in the mood for a latte." She smiled and took a sip.

I took a sip, too, and to my surprise, it wasn't bad. Before then, I hadn't seen myself chilling in a coffee shop sipping on an iced latte and having a conversation with a pretty girl. But then, I'd never seen myself as a college student before, either. My life was definitely taking a different route.

seven

Tameka

A baseball cap on my head and dark sunglasses on my eyes, I waddled through the mall in search of a shoe store. I was in desperate need of a new pair of sandals and some fresh air, which was why I allowed my friends to drag me out into public for the first time in months. The only place I'd been was my prenatal exercise classes that took place every Saturday morning, and everybody there was pregnant so there was no need in feeling out of place. Going to the mall was a different story, but my friends weren't taking no for an answer, and I had run out of excuses.

"Now aren't you glad you got out of the house?" Indigo asked. "Being stuck up in there can't be healthy for you *or* the baby."

"I agree," Asia added. "You were depressing me."

"What does it feel like? Being pregnant, I mean..." Jade asked.

"I don't know, like you're fat or something," I said. "I'm miserable when it's hot outside, which seems to be every day now. I'm depressed a lot. I can't fit into any of my clothes anymore, and then I look at you heifers and you all have on sexy shorts and cute little tops and I wanna strangle you."

"It's only temporary," Tymia encouraged. "After you have the baby, you'll have your body back."

"I don't even know my body anymore. It's like I don't know who I am anymore," I said. "And it's sad that I have to go through this alone. Mommy goes to my exercise classes with me. And she'll probably go with me to my Lamaze classes when they start, since Vance is not here."

"Lamaze?" Tymia said. "What's that?"

"They're childbirth classes," Indigo answered for me.

"Teach you how to breathe," I added.

"You don't know how to breathe?" Asia asked.

"Yes, silly, I'm talking about breathing during childbirth." I laughed. "You learn a lot of things at these classes. Like how to handle the pain of childbirth, too."

"Wow, pain…I don't know if I could handle the pain," Jade said. "I can't stand to get a paper cut."

"You?" Tymia said. "I can't even stand the sight of blood."

"You also watch childbirth videos and you learn about breast-feeding."

"Breast-feeding?" Indigo asked. "Are you going to breast-feed, Tameka?"

"Thinking about it," I said. "Breast milk is healthier for the baby."

"Won't it make your breasts sag like an old lady's?" Tymia asked.

"No. Who told you that?" I asked, not quite sure about it, even though I was pretending to be an authority on the subject. I hadn't really given much thought to the fact that my breasts might sag.

"It just seems like all that milk weighing your breasts down might make them sag. But I guess if the baby's sucking all the milk out of 'em, they might not sag so much," Tymia said.

"I heard that breast-feeding really hurts," Jade said.

"Can we change the subject?" I asked, and then stepped into the air-conditioned shoe store. With Vance's basketball jersey covering my swollen belly, and maternity shorts that crept up my backside, I went straight for a pair of leather sandals that had a clearance sign in front of them. I picked them up and observed the heel.

"Would you like to try them on?" the salesclerk asked.

"Yeah, let me see a size seven," I said. Then remembering that my feet were swollen and I had been borrowing Mommy's shoes, I added, "Better bring me an eight."

My friends started browsing through the store as I took a seat and waited for my shoes. Incognito behind my shades, I hadn't even seen Keisha Taylor from the dance team walk in. Wearing a tangerine-colored tank top and very short denim shorts, her fingers were intertwined with Chuck Brown's. Chuck was on the school's basketball team and had been her boyfriend since Christmastime. I hid my face as they walked past.

"Tameka, will you please tell this chick that Omarion is way finer than Bow Wow." Tymia and Asia were arm in arm as they approached, having an argument about something ridiculous. Blowing my cover.

Keisha's head swung my way. She'd obviously recognized Tymia and Asia.

"Hey y'all, what's up?" she asked.

"Hey, Keisha, I thought you were going to San Diego for the summer," Asia said.

I stood and walked away. Started browsing through the clearance rack, pretending to look at more shoes.

"Naw, plans changed a little bit," Keisha said. "I gotta go to summer school instead."

It seemed that she was following me around the store because within seconds she was on my heels.

"Is that you, Tameka Brown?" she asked. "Somebody told me you were pregnant."

Could she have said it any louder? It was as if everyone in the store stopped what they were doing and looked my way. My sunglasses hadn't been very good at hiding my identity or my embarrassment.

"Yeah, it's me."

"Wow, you're big," she said reaching for my stomach. "How many months are you?"

"Thirteen weeks," I answered reluctantly.

"How does that average in months?" she asked, not even realizing that she was all up in my business.

"You do the math," I said and then walked out of the store, not caring that the blond salesclerk was standing there with my size-eight sandals.

I walked and walked, without any destination in mind. I just needed to get out of the store and away from Keisha. I needed some fresh air and headed for the doors of the mall. I rushed outside and plopped down on the nearest bench. Something inside of me wanted to cry. I wished I was at home where I was safe—safe from all the nosy people who would judge me because I had made a mistake. They would judge me because I chose to keep my baby instead of aborting it. Who gave them the right to think they were better than me?

My phone started buzzing. No doubt it was my friends wondering where I'd disappeared to. I just needed to be alone. It was too soon to be out in public, and I'd tried explaining that to Indigo. She just didn't understand my situation. She wasn't the one who was pregnant—too big to fit into any of her clothes. She wasn't the one on an emotional roller coaster every single day, wishing her boyfriend would at least call and check on her.

I hadn't heard from Vance in three days. I'd stopped

leaving messages because he obviously wasn't interested in returning any of them. He was busy; I knew that, but he had no idea what I was dealing with—carrying his baby and not having any support from him. This was just as much his responsibility as it was mine. Yet I was the only one dealing with the consequences of it.

My phone buzzed again. I stared at the screen as Indigo's name flashed across it. I answered.

"Let's go," I said. "I'm ready to go home."

"Where are you?" she asked.

"I'm outside," I said. "Sitting on a stupid bench!"

I didn't mean to take it out on her—my anger, my hurt, my humiliation, but she just happened to be the one on the other end of the phone.

"We'll be right there," she said and then hung up.

The ride home was quiet as Asia maneuvered her mother's Chevy Malibu down Jonesboro Road. It seemed like the longest ride ever as she pulled into my driveway.

"Thanks for the ride," I said and opened my door.

"I'm gonna stay here," Indigo said and hopped out the car, too. "Y'all go ahead. I'll have my daddy pick me up later."

I didn't protest and didn't ask why she was staying. In a way, I was glad that Indigo decided to stay with me. I thought I wanted to be alone, but the truth was I needed the company. Needed to feel like my life was still just as normal as it always had been, as normal as my friends' lives. I needed to be that same old Tameka from the dance team, the one who could shake her booty better than the rest of them.

The two of us headed for my front porch and watched Asia put the car in reverse and pull out of the driveway. I opened the front door and we both stepped inside. After removing our shoes, we went upstairs to my room. I collapsed onto my bed. Indigo sat on the edge of the bed and grabbed my iPod.

"Sorry about the episode at the mall," I said. "When I saw Keisha I just lost it."

"It's okay. I understand," Indigo said. "I just wanted to make sure you were okay."

"I'm just not ready for the world to see me like this—all fat and out of shape. It's so embarrassing, waddling around the mall like this," I explained.

Indigo gave me a strange look. "You know you're going to have to get out there at some point, right?"

"I know. But I'm just not ready yet."

"School starts in August, Tameka. What're you going to do then? You can't hide in your house forever."

She had a point.

"I mean, it's not like you're the first teenage girl to get pregnant, Tameka. Everybody makes mistakes."

I didn't have a response. Everything she was saying was right. In fact, I'd already played the same thoughts in my head a million times. It didn't make waddling through the mall any easier, though.

"Look, girl." Indigo rubbed her palm against my stomach. "You have a baby growing in there. He or she needs you...."

"*She,*" I interrupted. I already knew the sex of the baby.

"She? For real?" she asked.

"Yeah, it's a girl."

"Cool!" Indigo exclaimed. "Well, *she* needs you right now. She doesn't need for you to be ashamed of her. You decided that you wanted to keep your baby instead of getting an abortion, right?"

"Yep," I said.

"So you gotta live with your decision. No matter what."

Her hand was still on my stomach when the baby kicked.

"Did you feel that?" I smiled.

"Was that a kick?" Indigo asked. "That girl is tripping! Acting like she's a football player instead of a dancer."

We both laughed. I was glad that Indi came home with me. I felt better with her being there—not so alone.

"Indi, will you go with me to my next exercise class?" I asked. "I love my mama to death, you know that. But she's not the best exercise partner. She's bossy."

"Mel's bossy?"

"Yeah, she's getting carried away with this baby. Making sure I eat right and stuff. I can't even have a Reese's Peanut Butter Cup in peace. And you know that's my favorite candy. And I better not even think about drinking an orange soda. She goes ballistic!"

"She's just making sure the baby's healthy."

"Yeah? Well she's driving me crazy," I said. "Acting like she's the one giving birth."

Indigo laughed and fell backward onto my bed next to me. We lay side by side, our eyes facing the ceiling. She grabbed my hand in hers; our fingers intertwined.

"Yep, I'll go to your exercise class with you. I'm here for you…whatever you need me to do."

"Thanks. Right now, I just need a friend."

We lay there in the middle of my bed, our eyes looking at the ceiling. We talked about everything under the sun—from our boyfriends, to dances that we did on the dance team, to fashion and how I can still look hot in maternity clothes. Getting through this time was going to be tough, but I felt better knowing that Indi had my back. Everything was going to be just fine.

eight

Vance

Dressed in a green polo shirt and a pair of denim shorts, I sprayed lots of cologne on my neck and chest. I rubbed my palm across my clean-shaven face and brushed my waves. I looked down at my green-and-white Jordans and knew that I looked good. I was just minutes away from my first frat party when my phone started ringing. I pulled it out of my pocket and gazed at the screen. Tameka. To answer it meant I'd have to explain why I hadn't called her since the day I arrived on campus. I'd have to explain that practices had me exhausted most days, and when I got some downtime she was the last person I wanted to talk to. All she ever wanted to talk about was the baby and her pregnancy and how she always felt bad. She always wanted to know where our relationship was headed, or if college was going to change things between us. She would kill my party mood.

I let it roll into voice mail. I promised myself that I'd call her after practice the next morning. The next morning would be Saturday, and after Saturday morning practice Jaylen and I had plans of cruising over to the mall just to check things out. There wouldn't be the stress of having to get to class and I could talk to Tameka in peace. She would have to wait until then, I thought as I rubbed lotion on my ashy legs. Before I could finish, my phone rang again. Tameka. Again. My heart began to pound. Something must be wrong if she's calling back-to-back like that, I thought. I stared at the screen for a moment, debating on whether or not I wanted to kill my mood. A frat party was calling my name, and the girls who had invited Jaylen and me to the party would be waiting for the dances that we promised them.

"Yo, what's up?" I asked as I picked up the phone.

"What's up with you?" Tameka asked. "Why haven't I heard from you, Vance?"

"I just been busy. With practice and everything. I don't have a lot of time on my hands, Tameka," I explained. "How you been doing, though?"

"Not good. This pregnancy thing is really hard for me, Vance. It's cramping my style. And then, I don't even hear from you anymore. It's like you just dropped off of the face of the earth when you went away to college," she whined. "Vance, what's up? I thought you said you would be there for me."

"I am here for you, Tameka. But I'm down here trying to play ball right now."

"Did you forget about me? Did you forget about the baby?" she asked.

"No, I didn't forget about you or the baby. I think about you every day."

"I can't tell, Vance. You don't call...you don't text. I'm just down here doing this by myself and I feel so alone sometimes."

"I'm sorry. I'll try and do better," I told her. I had to keep her calm, it was the best way. "You forgive me?"

There was a long pause—as if she was contemplating the answer.

"Yeah, I forgive you." Her voice was sweet again. Not nagging like it'd been earlier. She sounded like the Tameka that I'd fallen for in high school. The one who would kiss me and turn my world upside down. The one who was carrying my baby in her belly. A baby that neither of us were ready for. I was facing a new lifestyle that included dirty diapers and formula, not frat parties like the one I was headed to.

"Yo, man, let's go!" Jaylen burst through the door wearing khaki shorts and my red Coogi shirt. A Budweiser in his hand, he yelled, "You ready to party or what, dog?"

I shook my head no, giving him a clue that he should shut up. I pointed at the phone and he got the hint and covered his mouth as if to say *I'm sorry.* But it was too late.

"So, you on your way to a party?" Tameka asked, attitude in her voice.

"Yeah, they having this little frat party tonight. Me and Jaylen are thinking about checking it out," I admitted.

"So, you got time to make plans for a party, but you ain't got time to call and see how I'm doing?" she said. "So, you down there just kickin' it while I'm here pregnant, with swollen feet, can't even leave the house because I'm too ashamed that somebody might see me?"

"You got it all wrong. I'm not down here partying! This is my first party since I been here. Every day I'm at practice, and I don't even have time to grab a bite to eat before I collapse in my bed. I got summer classes and I barely have enough time to study," I explained. "Tameka, why you trippin'?"

"I'm not trippin', Vance. I just thought that you would be there for me. You promised me, but I don't even hear from you. And the first time I talk to you in weeks and you're on your way to a party."

"It's not that big of a deal. Some dudes on campus are trying to get me and Jaylen to join their fraternity, so we just checking things out," I said.

Jaylen tapped his watch to let me know that we needed to go.

"I gotta go, baby." I sighed. "But I promise I'll call you tomorrow after practice. And we can talk all day, okay?"

"You promise, Vance?" She was skeptical.

"I promise," I said and then went one step further. "I'll even text you when I get back to my dorm later...just to say good-night."

Jaylen shook his head no and made a motion like he was cutting his neck with a knife.

"Okay, baby. I'll be waiting to hear from you." Her voice was sweet again. "Tell big-headed Jaylen I said what's up."

"Okay, I'll tell him," I said. "I'll talk to you later."

I couldn't wait to hang up. Jaylen gave me a cockeyed look. "Why did you lie to that girl like that?"

"What?" I asked, playing dumb.

"You know good and well you ain't gon' text her when you get home tonight."

"I am," I said and headed for the door. "Tameka's my girl."

"I guess you forgot about the little honey that's waiting for you at the party. The one with the light eyes and the plump booty..."

"Tameka's still my girl," I insisted, trying to convince myself just as much as I was trying to convince Jaylen.

The truth was I hadn't stopped thinking about Lexi since the moment I saw her. I couldn't get the smell of her cologne out of my mind, and her eyes and banging body didn't help much, either. She kept creeping into my dreams at night; uninvited, of course. But not unwanted. We exchanged numbers under the pretense that she would help me with calculus, but as the text messages started flying back and forth, they were about everything but calculus.

Lexi was from Jackson, Mississippi, and was attending

Grambling on a basketball scholarship, just like me. She was the only girl in a family of five brothers, which explained why she was somewhat of a tomboy. Her schedule was hectic like mine, but we still managed to find time to text and talk at least twenty times over the course of a day. Each day when her camp was over, she'd wait for me outside the gym and I'd walk her to her dorm. I told myself time and again, "She's just a friend." There's no harm in walking a friend home from practice, and I actually had myself convinced of it until the day her lips touched mine for the first time. I wanted to stop it but I couldn't. Instead, I pulled her body closer to mine and actually wanted the moment to last forever.

As I lay in my twin bed that night, I was confused. I already had a girl. Tameka. In fact, I had a family. Tameka was carrying my baby and she was relying on me to be there for her. But I was too busy falling in love with someone else and I didn't know how to stop it. But I knew I had to. I had responsibilities. For two days, I avoided Lexi. When practice was over, I ducked into the locker room and didn't surface until I was sure she'd gone on without me. I needed to stay away from her. She caused things inside of me to be topsy-turvy. She caused me to feel things that I'd never felt before, and the inner struggle had my head messed up.

"Are you avoiding me?" she finally asked one day, cornering me after practice.

"Nah," I lied. "What makes you think that?"

"Well, I haven't heard from you in like two days...no phone calls...no text messages," she said, those beautiful eyes peering at me as if they could see into my soul. "I'm not sweating you or anything. I was just curious."

"Nah, I just been busy," I said and then changed the subject. "Where you headed?"

"To the cafeteria for some grub." She smiled that beautiful smile. "You coming?"

"Yeah, I'm coming," I said and started strolling beside her.

"I'll race you." Lexi started jogging slowly backward.

"You can't beat me, so don't even waste your time," I boasted.

"Come on then, let's see what you got," she taunted. She was competitive and I loved that about her. She wasn't soft like most girls.

"I don't wanna embarrass you," I said. I wanted to grab her right then and hold her in my arms.

"You don't wanna embarrass yourself." She laughed.

That did it. My male ego kicked in and I started running. Lexi started running, too, and almost caught me. But I was too quick for her. Bent over in front of the cafeteria, trying to catch my breath, I waited for her to show up.

"What took you so long?" I asked her.

"You cheated, Vance. You took off running before anybody said ready, set *or* go."

"No excuses, girl. I beat you fair and square."

"No you didn't," she insisted.

"Yes, I did," I wrapped my arm around Lexi's neck. I had to touch her, needed to be close to her. I put her in a headlock.

"I'm falling for you, V," she said, lifting her head, her eyes gazing into mine.

Why did she have to go there? Why did she have to verbalize what I was feeling for her, too? Didn't she know that my life was already complicated? Too complicated for conversations like this. Too complicated for strange feelings to be running through me like a freight train. Too complicated for her to be in my dreams every night.

"Come on, girl, let's go see what's on this menu," I said, avoiding her comment. Nobody needed to be falling for anybody, in my opinion. Especially since one of us had a girl-friend and a baby on the way. I had to constantly remind myself of that fact.

"It's probably burgers today," Lexi stated, not even flinching at the fact that I had avoided her comment. She went on as if nothing was ever said.

In my heart I wanted to say, "I'm falling for you, too, Lexi girl." But I knew better. Life was complicated enough, and who needed the hassle?

That was days ago. Tonight as I got dressed for the party, I couldn't wait to see her face.

Jaylen and I stepped into the party as Flo Rida's voice filled the room. People were all over the dance floor. Jaylen immediately started bouncing to the music. He smoothly made his way over to a light brown girl who was holding a bottle of beer in her hand, whispered something in her ear and instantly they were on the dance floor together. I moved to the music while I scanned the room, in search of that familiar face that belonged to Lexi. When skinny arms wrapped themselves around me from behind, I knew I'd found her.

"Who you looking for?" she asked.

I turned to face her. "You." I smiled and planted a kiss on her plump lips.

"Wanna dance?" she asked, and then pulled me onto the dance floor without waiting for an answer.

While moving to the beat of Flo Rida, I lived in the moment. There was no place I'd rather have been than where I was at that moment. Feeling that way seemed right, but everything in me told me it was wrong. As I watched Lexi shake her sexy body in front of me, everything became shades of gray. I didn't know the difference between right and wrong anymore.

nine

Marcus

Jae was staring at his computer screen when I stepped into the room. He looked at me and smiled.

"Hello, Marcus."

"What's up, Jae?" I asked and decided to have a little fun with my Korean roommate who could barely speak English. "You chillin' chillin'?"

"Chillin' chillin'?" he asked.

"Yeah, chillin'. You know, just hanging and being cool," I explained my slang to him.

"Being cool?"

"Yeah, chillin' and being cool. That's a good thing, Jae. It means that you're all right." I smiled. "I got a lot to teach you in just a few weeks."

"Tell me about your family, Marcus," Jae said. "Tell me about Georgia."

"Well, I live with my Pop...I mean, my father. He got custody of me after him and my mother got a divorce. My mother lives in Texas."

"You wanted to live with your father?"

"Well, I didn't really have a choice. My mother sort of walked out on us. She left us," I explained. "It was my father who took care of me when I was little. But my mother came back after a few years."

"Were you angry with her for leaving?" Jae asked.

"Yeah, I was pretty pissed off when she left."

Jae struggled to understand. "Pissed off?"

"Yeah, I was upset. That's what pissed off means...you know, angry. She left me at a time in my life when I really needed her."

"Do you have siblings?"

"Nah, I'm an only child," I said. "What about you, Jae? You got sisters and brothers?"

"I have five sisters and one brother. I am the youngest child of seven. My parents are very poor. Much poverty in my country. I am the first to attend college," Jae said.

"Well, that's cool." I smiled.

"Yes, cool." Jae smiled. "Chillin' chillin'. Right, Marcus?"

I nodded and laughed. That's all I could do as I dropped my shoes and relaxed on my bed.

"I miss my girl," I said. "I miss her like crazy."

"You have a girlfriend?" he asked. "What is her name?"

"Indigo," I said and pulled her picture from the drawer of my nightstand. Showed it to Jae. "This is her."

"She's very pretty." He grabbed the photo and stared at it for a moment. Handed it back to me.

"Yeah, she is," I said and then tucked her picture back into its place. "What about you, Jae? You got a girl back home in Korea?"

He was silent for a moment then dropped his head.

"Yes, but we can't be together. Our families have too much hatred for one another. Our fathers are too stubborn." Jae's eyes were sad. "I love her, but our love is forbidden."

"What? That sound like some Romeo and Juliet type stuff, man."

"Romee and Julie? Who's that?"

"Romeo and Juliet. It's an old story by an old writer, William Shakespeare, about two lovers who couldn't be together because of their families. It's pretty sad."

"I never read that story before," Jae said. "Where can I find it?"

"Go to the library. It's probably in there," I told him.

"You think it's there?" he asked.

"I'm sure it is," I said. "It's like a classic story. Every library in the world probably has it on the shelf."

"Will you go with me, Marcus…to the library to find it?"

"Right now?"

"Yes. I would really like to read that story."

Was he serious? He wanted me to get up out of my comfortable bed and trample over to the Fine Arts Library in search of an ancient story.

"All right, man." I slipped my shoes back on to my feet. "Let's go."

We had to hurry. It was eight thirty-five by my watch, and the library closed at nine. We rushed over and just made it before closing. We both stood in front of the woman at the front desk; her head was down as she read something. When she looked up, I realized it was Daria.

"Hi." I smiled at her.

"Hi." She smiled back and we both just got lost in the moment.

Jae nudged me.

"Um…we're looking for William Shakespeare's *Romeo and Juliet,*" I said. "Can you help us find it?"

"Sure." She punched some buttons on her computer and then stood. "This way."

I watched her walk as she made her way to the fiction section of the library, Jae and I following close behind her. She went right to the book, pulled it from the shelf.

"*Romeo and Juliet?*" she asked. "You got a paper to write or something?"

"It's for my friend here." I nodded toward Jae. "He's never read it before."

"You'll need lots of tissue." She smiled at Jae. He smiled back, but it was clear he had no idea what she was talking about.

"Thank you," he responded.

"Marcus, I had a good time the other day," she said as she began walking back to the front of the library.

"Yeah, it was cool," I said, trying to keep the conversation light. Didn't really want to talk about anything personal in front of Jae. We followed Daria to the checkout counter where he placed his book.

"What are you doing tomorrow night?" she continued. "You wanna go to a party?"

"Sounds like fun," I said.

"Good. Let me give you my number." She grabbed a piece of paper from a notepad and jotted her number down on it. "Call me and we'll meet outside your dorm."

I grabbed the paper reluctantly from her fingertips. Stuffed it into the pocket of my jeans.

"Holler at you later," I said before ushering Jae out the door.

I was grateful for air as we stood outside the library and headed back toward our dorm.

"What was that?" Jae asked.

"What was what?" I played dumb.

"Was she flirting with you…or were you flirting with her? And did she just ask you to go on a date?" He grinned. "What about Indigo?"

"What are you talking about, man? Nobody was flirting. And it's not a date, it's just a party. And she's just a friend."

"Just a friend." Jae laughed and then mocked Daria. "I

had a good time the other day, Marcus." He batted his eyes like a girl would. "What was that?"

"It was nothing. We just went to a coffee shop, had a couple of lattes," I explained.

"Lattes?"

"It's coffee, man!" I was becoming irritated.

"She's very beautiful." He grinned. "And you said *'it was cool.'* That is a good thing, right?"

"Come on, Jae. You got a lot to learn about American girls and about life."

"Love is universal, Marcus," he said, "no matter what country you are in."

"I love my girlfriend back home, Indigo. I promise you that."

"But you're attracted to the beautiful lady in the library. No?"

"She's pretty. Okay, there. I admitted that she's pretty," I said. "Now can we talk about something else? Tell me about this forbidden lover of yours."

"Joo-Eun?" he asked, as if I already knew her name. "She's very beautiful. I've known her since we were both five years old. Our families have known each other a long time. My father worked for her father, and they were once good friends."

"What happened to make them not be friends any-more?" I asked.

"It's a long story. Too many bad things...too much pain."

"But you're in love with...what's her name?" I asked.

"Joo-Eun," he said. "But she has been promised to someone else. She will marry soon."

"Are you for real? How old is this girl?"

"She's fifteen. It is customary in Korea for the father of the bridegroom to choose a wife for his son. And he has chosen Joo-Eun."

"That's crazy. So, you don't even get a say in the matter?

You just gotta let your girl go marry some other dude like that?" I asked. "Can't you fight for her?"

"It's senseless. I cannot win. I will love her silently for the rest of my life, and will go to my grave knowing that I love her and she loves me."

"That's sad, bro," I said, really feeling Jae's pain. "I'm glad that in America I can choose who I want to be with. And if I don't like her, I can move on to someone else. No place like the U.S. of A, man."

Jae and I made our way back to the dorm. I kicked my shoes off once again. Jae did a nosedive into the book, *Romeo and Juliet*, and stayed there for hours, reading silently in his bed. I sent a text message to Indigo.

WUP?

Nothin, she responded.

Go swimming 2day?

Went 2 da mall wit my girlz.

Where u at?

Spendin da nite at Tameka's. She needs a friend.

Is she big as a house?

Just a little. Be nice.

Sorry…she's preggers right?

She's sad…Vance is trippin.

He's 17…what does she expect?

A father for her baby!

Both are too young for dat.

Where's Jay? she asked, spelling his name wrong.

I had told Indigo about Jae; told her about the communication barrier that we had on the first day, but that I thought he was a nice guy. And that I would school him.

Jae is reading Romeo & Juliet.

?? She was confused.

Long story…get sum z's…call u 2morrow.

K...g'nite.

It was good to know that Indigo was still under my skin, still the girl who invaded my dreams. Still my one and only Indigo Summer.

ten

Tameka

indigo and I took the elevator up to the twenty-fifth floor. I stood in the corner, dressed in stretch pants and Vance's extra-large basketball shirt with Armstrong, his last name, plastered across the back of it. He'd left it in our garage one day when he came over for a visit. That was the day that he'd challenged me to a game of one-on-one at the goal in front of my neighbor's house. Back then I was much smaller, in better shape and not pregnant. It was before my ankles were swollen and before my thighs were the size of ham hocks.

I'd chosen braids for the summer, an easier style to maintain. I grabbed a handful of braids and pulled them back on my head with a scrunchy. I looked over at Indigo, who was dressed in tight leotards like the ones we wore in dance practice, a long T-shirt and sneakers. She glanced over at me and smiled.

"You okay?" she asked.

"Yep, I'm cool."

Saturday morning prenatal exercise classes were always fun. I loved the exercises and the positive energy that filled the room. I was a dancer and used to exercising so it was important for me to stay in shape, even during pregnancy.

The instructor taught that doing prenatal exercises would make childbirth much easier. Also, it would help keep the pounds under control after the baby was born. For me, it was a way of hanging out with people who were just like me—pregnant—and not feeling embarrassed about it. I had made new friends. Even though I was the youngest in the class, I still connected with the older women who gave me advice and support.

Patricia was twenty-one and pregnant by her thirty-five-year-old, very married boyfriend. Her mother kicked her out of the house the minute she found out about the pregnancy. She was left with nowhere to go and had ended up on the street for a few days. Her aunt finally took her in, but she had to work to pay rent, and because the house was overcrowded, she had to share a bedroom with three other people. There was barely anything left to eat at home by the time she got off from her minimum-wage-paying job at Kentucky Fried Chicken, and many nights she went to bed hungry. The woman at the WIC office told her about a program where she could get free milk, juices and other food for free because of her income. She also told her about the exercise class. It was a way of escape for her. And even though her aunt complained about the class being a waste of time, she made a commitment to show up every single Saturday.

Jolene was the mother of three and was carrying her fourth child. Her husband was a truck driver and was barely at home. He was upset when he found out that Jolene was pregnant again—complaining that it was hard enough feeding the children that they already had. He accused her of not being honest about her birth control. She was convinced that her husband would change his attitude once he laid eyes on the baby when it was born. I hoped he would, too, because Jolene was very sweet. With her dark brown skin and long flat-ironed hair, she was the first person to approach me on the first day of class. She gave me good advice about being a young mother; told me that she was seventeen when she'd had her first baby. She encouraged me to stay positive. Her mother volunteered to watch the kids on Saturday mornings so that she could attend classes. And she jumped at the chance every single week, just to get a break from the little rugrats.

Deja was happily married to Arnold. He dropped her off every Saturday morning and gave her big hugs and kisses before he disappeared across town to play basketball with his homeboys. Deja and Arnold had both graduated from Clark Atlanta University. Arnold was an engineer and Deja worked as an intern for a major law firm while she attended law school. I admired Deja. In fact, I often imagined Vance and I being just like Deja and Arnold. We would both attend college and end up with great careers. We would get married and build a nice house in Gwinnett County just like them. And we would have a great life—Vance, the baby and me.

Fawn was an older woman with a seventeen-year-old son. With her flawless skin and short and sassy haircut, she looked way too young to have a son that age. She reminded me of my mother; very fashionable and modern. They had instantly become friends when they met at one of our exercise sessions. They were already planning trips to the mall, and Fawn even joined my mother's book club. She was pregnant by a man who she'd only dated for a short time. When she told him that she was pregnant he didn't seem to care, and in fact he broke off the relationship, stating that he wasn't ready to be a father again. His kids were grown and he wasn't ready to be changing diapers and warming formula at this stage in his life. It left Fawn pretty much alone, but her son kept her company most of the time.

Indigo and I stepped out of the hospital elevator and into the room where a few people had already started to gather. Some of them sat around the room nibbling on fresh fruits.

"Hey, Tameka girl!" Jolene said as I walked into the room. "Your belly looks a little rounder today."

"Hey, everybody." I smiled at my pregnant friends as they gobbled down chunks of watermelon, pineapple and bananas.

It was not unusual for Deja's husband, Arnold, to be in our classroom. He often walked her to class and kissed her goodbye at the door. But this morning I noticed another strange man standing near the food, popping chunks of fruit into his mouth like there was no tomorrow.

"Tameka, come here, honey." Fawn rushed toward me, grabbed me by the hand and dragged me across the room. "I got somebody I want you to meet…"

The strange man set his plate down and looked my way as we approached.

"Tameka, this is my son, Sean." She smiled. "Sean, this beautiful young lady is Tameka."

"How you doing, Tameka?" Sean's voice was deep for a seventeen-year-old. He was tall and slender with dark brown skin and a short haircut. Wearing denim shorts and a tall tee, he reached his hand out.

"I'm fine, thanks." I shook his hand.

"Isn't he just the cutest?" Fawn pinched Sean's cheek.

"Ma, please!" Sean groaned.

"Sean's mad because I made him come to class with me today," Fawn said, "but I didn't feel like driving this morning, so he didn't have much of a choice."

Sean rolled his eyes and grabbed another piece of watermelon. Popped it into his mouth.

"It was nice meeting you," I said before joining Indigo at the other side of the room.

"I am loving these braids." Deja ran her fingers through my hair.

"Thank you," I told her. "It's too hot for anything else."

"You got that right. I'm getting ready to get me some braids." Patricia rubbed her belly. "Who's your friend?"

"Oh, my bad. This is my friend, Indigo," I said. "Indi, this is Deja and that's Patricia."

"Hi." They all said it in unison.

I pulled Indigo to the other side of the room.

"And this is Fawn," I said. "Fawn, this is my friend, Indigo."

"Nice to meet you, honey," Fawn said and grabbed Indigo's hand.

"You, too," said Indi.

"And this is Sean. He's Fawn's son."

"Hi." Indigo smiled.

"What's up?" Sean said and then went back to text messaging someone from his phone.

As Beyoncé's "Single Ladies (Put A Ring On It)" echoed through the room, Patricia started shaking to the music. Our instructor, Ruby, entered the room wearing a sports bra and low-rise workout shorts. Her abs were tight and her calves toned. Each week I wanted to grab her chiseled body and drag it down the street. It was a crime for her body to look like that in front of a bunch of pregnant women. It was hard to believe that she'd just given birth less than a year before.

She often gave us lectures about how important it was to exercise during our pregnancies, and especially after the baby was born. She showed us pictures of when she was pregnant, as well as flashing photos of little Kianna, her ten-month-old baby girl. Ruby taught us how to eat, exercise and care for our bodies from head to toe.

"Okay, ladies, let's get started!" she said. Always full of energy, she bounced around the room. "Let's do our stretches."

All of us stretched our oversize bodies onto the floor and began pulling muscles that didn't want to be pulled. Indigo plopped down on the floor next to Deja and did the same stretches as the rest of us. We were used to working out together; it's what we did in Miss Martin's dance class every single day. Neither of us were strangers to physical training.

"Okay, let's pair off and do our usual exercises," Ruby announced. "Go ahead and get paired up with the person next to you."

Since there was an odd number of people in the room, pairing up left me without a partner. Indigo was quickly whisked away by Deja. I shrugged as Ruby looked my way. I wasn't necessarily looking forward to pairing with her. She was like Miss Martin in many ways, a workhorse. She was a perfectionist and I wasn't in the mood for perfection today. I would've preferred doing my exercises alone, but she never allowed that.

"Young man," she called to Fawn's son. "May I see you for a moment?"

Sean looked up from his cell phone.

"His name is Sean," Fawn announced and smiled.

"Sean, can you lend us a hand over here please?" she asked. "Tameka doesn't have a partner. Will you be her partner for a little while?"

Was she serious? I could feel my face turning beet red with embarrassment as he looked my way.

Sean shrugged, stuffed his phone into his pocket. "Okay."

He made his way over and stood in front of me.

"Great!" Ruby was too bubbly in the morning sometimes. "Let's get started."

We started doing a series of arm and upper back stretches, pelvic tilts, sit-ups, squatting and calf stretches. Sean offered support as I did my exercises, making sure that I didn't hurt myself. He was there in case I needed help sitting up or squatting. At one point I squatted and had trouble standing. When Sean tried to pull me up from the floor, I pulled him down instead. Falling onto the floor, we both fell out in laughter.

Taking a break, Sean and I sat in the middle of the floor.

"So, what are you, like fifteen or sixteen?"

Here comes the embarrassing part, I thought.

"I'm almost seventeen," I said.

"Where's your baby's father?" he asked.

"He's in college. He just left for summer school a few weeks ago," I said. "Got a basketball scholarship."

"That's cool," he said. "I'm going to college in the fall, too. Georgia State."

"Really?" I smiled. "You play ball?"

"Nah," he said.

"What will you major in?" I asked.

"I'm not really sure yet. I'll figure it out later," he said. "My moms wants me to be an architect, but I don't know about that. I'm a musician really."

"What kind of music do you do?"

"I play the keyboards…by ear," he boasted. "And I rap. That's what I'm trying to do. I'm trying to get on somebody's label. Matter of fact, I'm not even really feeling school. I'm just going because that's what she wants."

He glanced over at Fawn.

"Well, it's gotta be about what you want," I encouraged. "Can you flow?"

"Of course I can." He smiled and then started free-styling.

He flowed nicely and I was impressed. His sound was original and I liked what I heard.

"That was good," I said.

"You really think so?" he asked.

"Mos def," I said.

"Thank you," he said.

He seemed to really need the encouragement and I was glad that I could help out. When our short break was over, he pulled me up from the floor—successfully this time. We finished off the next set of exercises, Sean helping me out until we were done.

"Thank you for being my partner, Sean," I said.

"It was my pleasure." The ringing of his phone interrupted us. He walked away as he answered.

Indigo found her way over to me.

"Well, that was fun." She wiped sweat from her forehead.

"This is what we do every Saturday," I explained.

"You should come back next week," Deja told Indigo.

"I just might," Indi said.

"Nice to meet you, Indigo." Patricia waddled toward us. "You have a good week, Tameka. And I'll see you next Saturday."

"Okay." We embraced.

"See you later, Tameka," Fawn said. "Are you coming back again, Indi?"

"I'll probably come back next week."

Fawn got closer to me, whispered in my ear, "I think Sean's a little sweet on you."

"What? No." I laughed.

"I'll see you next week, honey." Fawn winked and then walked toward the door. "Let's go, Sean."

I watched him, wondered if he would look my way so that I could say goodbye. After all, we had shared an interesting conversation. He had even freestyled for me. He never looked my way. With the cell phone pressed against his ear, he followed his mother out the door. Indigo locked arms with mine and we headed toward the door.

"He's cute." She smiled as she watched me watch him.

I didn't even bother to ask who or to expound on the conversation. I just ignored her and walked toward the elevators.

"Thanks for coming with me today. I really appreciate it."

"Not a problem," she said. "Now can we stop and get a smoothie, please?"

"Of course," I said and felt my phone buzz.

It was Vance. He called just as he promised. This was turning out to be a better day than I expected.

eleven

Vance

practice was the worst ever. It was hard trying to do physical activity with a pounding headache—or should I say *hangover*. The more beers I drank, the more they kept coming. Chauncey and Harlen made sure that Jaylen and I had the time of our lives. After practice, I called Tameka, just to let her know that I was capable of keeping a promise.

"What you doing?" I asked.

"Just leaving my exercise classes. Indi went with me today." She seemed to be in a much better mood than I was.

"That's cool. I'm glad you had support," I said.

"How was the party last night?" she asked.

"It was okay." That was a lie. It was the best party I'd ever been to in my life! But I hid my enthusiasm. Didn't want to hurt Tameka's feelings or set her off. It was nothing for her emotions to be out of whack.

"Was it a lot of girls there?"

"Yeah, it was girls there, Tameka. It was a party. What kind of question is that?" I laughed.

"You dance with anybody?" she asked.

"I danced a couple of times. Yeah."

The truth was, I stayed on the dance floor most of the night because Lexi was definitely a dancer. She was like the Energizer Bunny. She didn't quit. And it was hard just keeping up with her. We finally took a break and ended up in a quiet little spot outside, where I held her and shielded her from the night air. We talked about everything under the sun—everything except for my girl at home, Tameka, and the fact that she's pregnant. I couldn't bring myself to tell Lexi everything. I was afraid. Afraid that she would walk away before I had the chance to get to know her better.

She spilled her guts about the dude that she'd left behind in Mississippi. It seemed that they grew up together and their parents were the best of friends. It was their parents who insisted that they date each other, but the truth was, she didn't really like him like that. He wasn't her type, and she was so happy when she got the scholarship to Grambling. It was her escape; escape from parents who tried to run her life. And escape from Tyrone, the dude who wished he could hold her like I did. The dude who wished she would look into his eyes like she did mine. The dude who was stuck in Washington DC, at Howard University while the girl of his dreams was here in Louisiana falling in love with me.

"Who did you dance with?" Tameka asked.

"I don't really know their names. Just a couple of girls." I sat up in bed. "Hey, I gotta run right now. I need to go find something to eat. I just wanted to call you and check on you…like I said I would. I'll hit you back later."

"You promise?"

"Yeah, I promise."

Sometimes talking to Tameka was like pulling teeth, or sitting through a lecture from my parents, or struggling to stay awake in class—it was something that needed to be done but wasn't always easy. She made it hard for me. My mind drifted back to that night at her house when her parents were out of town—the night we made love for the first and last time. I had used protection, but it seemed that it wasn't enough to prevent her from getting pregnant. Condoms were never one hundred percent effective—they were more like ninety-nine percent effective. But they had never failed me before; they always seemed to protect me. But this one time, ninety-nine percent just wasn't enough. It was that one percent that got in the way—changed our lives forever.

My phone buzzed and interrupted my thoughts. It was Lexi. I picked up.

"Talk to me," I said.

"Still hung over?" she asked.

"I'm cool."

"I'm headed to the mall. You wanna hang out?"

My head was pounding and my body felt as if a tractor trailer had run over it. I was starving and a couple of extra hours of sleep would've been good. But the thought of seeing Lexi again made my heart race. Hanging out with her was better than anything else I could think of. She brought sunshine into my day.

"Let me hop in the shower and I'll meet you in about thirty minutes," I found myself saying.

"I'll be waiting."

Lexi leaned on the hood of a black Kia Sportage in the parking lot where she asked me to meet her. She was wearing a cropped top that showed off her pierced navel, a pair of denim capris and flip-flops.

"Whose car?" I asked.

"My friend Jessie's. She let me borrow it." She walked around to the driver's side of the car, hopped inside.

I hopped into the passenger's seat, immediately started adjusting the radio and stumbled upon the hip-hop station,

106. Lil Wayne's voice filled the car as Lexi headed for Pecanland Mall. The air in Jessie's car didn't work, so we let the windows all the way down just to catch a cool breeze. It was hot in Louisiana in June, very similar to Atlanta summers—the type of heat that made you want to jump into a pool of water just to keep cool.

At the mall, Lexi and I strolled past Foot Locker, and I popped my head into my favorite shoe store just to check out the latest in footwear. After browsing for a minute, Lexi pulled me away and into some girlie store where she seemed to find her home—trying on at least four pairs of jeans, two or three dresses. We stopped at a women's shoe store where she tried on several pairs of shoes. She tried on at least ten pairs of sunglasses at one of the mall's kiosks before settling on a pair with pink lenses to match the shirt that she wore.

"You are a shopper, for real, girl." I laughed as we strolled through the doors of the mall and headed for the parking lot. My hands filled with her shopping bags, I said, "I don't know if I can come back to the mall with you."

"What?" She acted as if she didn't know what I was talking about, took a sip of her smoothie. "I needed some stuff."

"You needed all this stuff?" I asked.

"All of it. The jeans were on sale, and fall is coming soon. Gonna need those for school," she explained. "And as far as the shoes, I can't wear flip-flops when it starts to get cold, right?"

"I guess not." I laughed.

Lexi hit the power locks and we both hopped into the hot car, the black leather burning our skin.

"Where does a college student get so much money to just kick around like that anyway?" I asked.

"I worked all through my senior year last year. My parents

are always complaining about money, so I saved my own before I left for college. I got a pretty nice little bank account."

"That's cool," I said. "My parents gave me a credit card, but I can only use it for emergencies. In the fall, I plan on getting me a job somewhere…just so I can have my own cash."

"You have to," she agreed. "I refuse to be a cliché—a broke college student. Daddy's always talking about his college days and how he had to eat ramen noodles and canned soup that he warmed over a hot plate in his dorm. That will not be me."

"Yeah, I heard those stories before, too," I told her. "Both my parents talked about being broke in college."

"What do your parents do for a living?" she asked.

"My moms is a lawyer. And my father is a dentist."

"That's cool. My mother is a schoolteacher. My father works for General Motors. He recently got laid off, so money is tight for us right now. It's a good thing I got this basketball scholarship," she said.

"I feel you. Getting a scholarship is priceless," I told her.

"I'm thinking about going home for the Fourth of July. What about you?"

"Nah, I'm not going home until Thanksgiving. Maybe even Christmas, depending…" I told her. The truth was, Tameka was due sometime in November and it was very likely I would be going home for the birth of my kid.

"Depending on what?" she asked.

"I don't know…just depending…" I said. "Depending on how I feel around that time."

"Well on the Fourth of July every year, my family has this big family reunion-type thing in Jackson. Relatives come from all over and my Daddy barbecues and we play all sorts of games like tug-of-war and baseball, and we have balloon fights. It's a lot of fun. You should come."

"You for real?" I couldn't help getting excited. It sounded fun and I felt privileged that she invited me.

"Yeah, for real," she said.

"Nah, I can't. I'm down here with my boy, Jaylen. I couldn't just run off to Mississippi and leave him here by himself. He wouldn't know what to do without me."

"So bring him," she said. "There's plenty of room at my parents' house for everybody. We can all just hang out there. As long as I let them know ahead of time that I'm bringing some friends home."

"I'll think about it."

"You for real?" she asked. "You should come for real, Vance. It'll be fun."

"I said I would think about it." I smiled at Lexi.

She didn't know it, but my mind had been made up the minute she asked. It sounded like too much fun to pass up.

"I'm hungry, Vance. Are you?" she asked.

"Yeah, I'm really hungry. What you feel like?"

"There's a place called the Rib Shack in Ruston. You eat barbecue?"

"Of course," I said. "Who doesn't?"

Lexi hopped on I-20 headed west toward Ruston, the radio on full blast as the wind blew through the windows. Finally pulling into the parking lot of the barbecue spot, we stepped from the car. Lexi's long windblown hair made her even more beautiful. I held the door as we stepped into the place. The smell of barbecue had my stomach growling—loud.

"Was that your stomach?" Lexi asked.

"I told you I was hungry." I laughed and held on to my stomach.

Lexi placed her hand over my stomach as if trying to see if I was really hungry or not. As the palm of her hand massaged my belly, I wrapped my arm around her neck and we scanned the menu. We ordered and found a table against the wall. Ate like there was no tomorrow and then headed back to Grambling.

As we walked hand in hand to her dorm, I pulled her knuckles up to my lips. Kissed them.

"I had a good Saturday," I told her.

"Me, too." She smiled. "Can we have a good Sunday, too?"

"And Monday, Tuesday, Wednesday..."

"You won't get tired of me?"

How could I get tired of a girl who was constantly in my dreams? Whenever I was apart from her, I couldn't wait to see her again. I couldn't imagine getting tired of her.

"Nah, not right away," I teased. "Maybe I will later."

"Think about the Fourth of July, okay?"

"I will." I handed Lexi her bags from the mall and she took off walking toward her dorm.

"Let me know soon, okay?"

"I will." I smiled as I watched her sexy body sashay down the sidewalk.

"I'll text you later."

"You do that."

I watched as she disappeared through the doors. Continued to watch, as if she might come back outside. I missed her already. And even as I began to jog backward in the opposite direction, I had an urge to call her cell phone just to say hi. What was up with this inner struggle of mine? What I wanted and what I had were two totally different things, and I didn't know how to balance the two.

twelve

Marcus

Daria and I stepped into one of the largest party suites on campus, with its slanted skylights and built-in bar. The music was loud as the sound of Jay-Z's voice echoed through the room. I'd never been to a party where I was the minority. Besides Daria and me, there was only one other African American person there. It was nothing like the high school parties I attended in College Park. It was way more grownup, with people standing around the room holding on to the necks of beers and wine coolers. There was never alcohol at the parties I went to back home.

I tried not to snicker as I watched white people dance to hip-hop. Instead I followed Daria across the room and we each grabbed a bottle of water from a cooler.

"I'm sure this is not like the parties you go to back home, Marcus," Daria said and smiled, "but it's something to do, right?"

"Will some other black people show up?"

"Probably not." She laughed. "But if you feel uncomfortable we can go."

"Nah, I'm cool," I told her as I stood against the wall, bounced my head to the music and took a drink of water.

"Marcus, old chap. How are you?" Paul asked and extended his hand for a shake.

"Hey, what's up?" I said, giving him a handshake.

Derrick grinned and extended his hand, too. "Marcus… what's up? You decided to show up. What brings you to the Bell Tower?" he asked, referring to the suite. "I thought this party was by invitation only."

"Well…I was invited." I grinned. "By my friend Daria here. Daria, this is Paul and Derrick."

"Nice to meet you both," Daria said and shook both their hands. "Marcus, I'll be right back. I see some people I know."

"Okay, do your thing," I told her.

She walked away and the three of us checked her out— all at the same time. Wearing a short, almost see-through dress and flat sandals, she looked as if she belonged at a photo shoot in Tahiti somewhere.

"She is fine," Derrick commented. "That you, man?"

"Nah, she's just a friend," I said.

"Hook me up, then." Derrick grinned.

I don't know why, but I was immediately jealous at the thought of Derrick being hooked up with Daria. I searched for an excuse to get his interest off of her.

"I don't know, man. She got this boyfriend that she talks about all the time," I lied. "I'll see what I can do. Can't make any promises, though."

"If her boyfriend's not here…at Harvard, then he doesn't matter." He smiled. "She's fair game."

Paul and Derrick drank beers as the three of us chitchatted about everything under the sun and listened to music. When Chris walked up, I wanted to walk away. Our first encounter in the dining hall hadn't been a pleasant one, and even though we were roommates, he wasn't one of my favorite people.

"Hello, good men. What's the word?" he asked and shook Paul's and Derrick's hands. He reached for mine. "Malcolm, is it?"

"Marcus," I corrected him.

"Close enough." He grinned, winked and took a drink from his cocktail. "This party is lame. I know a better party that's just a train ride from here. Anybody interested?"

"Anything has to be better than this," Derrick said.

"Paul, you interested?" Chris asked.

"I don't know. It's still early for this party. It'll probably get better later," Paul said.

"Don't count on it," Chris said.

"What about you, Marcus? You wanna take a ride?" Paul asked me, as if my answer would determine whether or not he joined Chris. "I'll go if you go."

"I don't know, man. I came here with Daria," I told him.

"Bring her along," Derrick said.

"Let me see if she's interested," I told them and then made my way across the room to where Daria was laughing with two other girls. I tapped her lightly on the arm. "Hey, Daria…"

"Hey, Marcus, what's up?" she asked.

"Me and a few of the fellas are going to another party…."

"Where?" she interrupted.

"I don't know…somewhere Chris knows about. He said we can take the train," I explained. "You wanna come?"

"Hmm." She smiled. "It sounds like fun."

She said a few more words to the girls she was chitchatting with and then followed me back to where Chris, Paul and Derrick were waiting. The five of us headed for the elevator, Chris leading the way. We walked across Harvard Yard, down the sidewalk toward the train station and hopped on the "T."

"Where are we going?" Derrick asked.

"I know a bar where we can all get in without ID," Chris stated.

"On what planet?" I asked. I was barely seventeen and my chance of getting into an adult bar was slim to none.

"Trust me." Chris grinned.

That was exactly what we did; trusted him. And soon we were pushing our way through a crowd of intoxicated partygoers. Soon I found myself dancing, too, with Daria moving her hips in front of me. Without words, we were in tune with each other, dancing as if we had practiced beforehand. She was a good dancer. She moved like she belonged on Miss Martin's dance team with Indigo and her girls.

To my left, Paul and Derrick found spots against the wall, where they stood and checked out the crowd. Chris had already grabbed a beer from the bar and was moving offbeat in front of a blonde girl who was tossing her hair from side to side. Wearing a bikini top and denim shorts that showed too much thigh for the public to see, she was aggressive. She grabbed Chris's beer and took a drink from it.

After the song ended, Daria grabbed my hand in hers and escorted me to the back of the bar. A couple of empty spots were available on a leather sofa, and we rushed over and grabbed them. Daria sat very close to me and crossed her silky, clean-shaven legs in front of me.

"This place is hot!" she said.

I nodded in agreement as Soulja Boy's voice suddenly rang out across the room. When the waitress approached, I ordered Cokes for Daria and me and hoped I had enough in my wallet to cover it. I had already spent twenty dollars getting us into the place. The cover charge was a small detail that Chris forgot to mention before we got there. I glanced over at him as he bounced around the room with Bikini Top.

He was in a zone and totally out of character. He wasn't the sarcastic, anal Chris who made inappropriate comments to total strangers—he was suddenly the party animal Chris who was putting away beers like a real alcoholic.

"What's his story?" Daria asked as Chris danced his way to the bar.

"Just recently met him," I said. "All I know is he's from Yellowknife, Idaho."

"He's wild." She smiled. "But I like the place he picked. This is cool."

"Yeah, it is."

The deejay slowed things down a little with some Keyshia Cole. Derrick and Paul headed our way. Paul grabbed an empty seat next to us. Derrick gave Daria a lustful look.

"Wanna dance?" he asked.

"Okay," she said, not realizing that he had more than dancing on his mind.

She followed him to the dance floor, his hand touching her lower back. She wrapped her arms around his neck as they slow danced to the music. A tinge of jealousy rushed through me as I watched Derrick grab a hold of her small waist. She was beautiful, I thought, as I watched her move to the music. Her face was a flawless light brown, her breasts were perfectly sized and her legs were the best parts on her body.

"She's gorgeous," Paul commented, obviously he'd busted me watching Daria way too close, "but Derrick is not her type."

"She might give him a shot," I said. My mouth said those words but my heart hoped they weren't true.

"Nah, he doesn't have a chance with a girl like that." Paul smiled. "She has eyes for someone else…you."

"I have a girl at home," I quickly said; reeled my feelings back in—focused on Indigo. "We're in a committed relationship."

"How committed can you be when she's in Georgia and you're in Cambridge, and a girl like that is dancing around in your dreams?"

How did he know that she was in my dreams? He had a point, though—a point that I hadn't considered before then. I was headed back to Atlanta in a few weeks, but soon I'd be leaving for Harvard again—for good. Where would that leave Indigo and me in the future? I had my goals and aspirations and she had hers. She was unsure about where she wanted to go to school—one day it was Spelman and the next day it was New York University—but every day it was something different.

"Marcus, you wanna dance now?" Daria was suddenly standing in front of me, taking a drink from her soda and pulling me onto the dance floor before I had a chance to protest.

Derrick looked as if he'd been slapped in the face as I followed Daria to the dance floor.

"What's up? You didn't like dancing with my boy, Derrick?" I asked her.

"Marcus, give me a break. I wanted to give him a mint, because his breath was kickin'!" She laughed. "While he was all up in my face trying to get my number."

"What? You didn't give him your number?" I teased.

"Marcus, shut up." She smiled that beautiful smile and part of me was relieved that she and Derrick didn't hit it off.

She moved in close to me, placed her hands on my chest. I grabbed her waist. Her hands moved to my face, caressed it. Her eyes gazed into mine, and it was perfectly natural for her lips to accidentally press themselves against mine. She opened her mouth and my tongue found its way inside—her peppermint kisses were refreshing. What was I doing with this girl in my arms—kissing her, as if she belonged to me? Someone was supposed to stop this from happening. Derrick looked as if he wanted to, but he couldn't. Indigo was nowhere to be found—not even in my thoughts. All I could think of was this brown beauty in front of me.

The place was suddenly chaotic. A crowd of people gathered as someone caused a ruckus near the men's room. People bumped against us as they rushed to see what the commotion was. Daria and I rushed over, only to find Chris in the middle of a brawl with four dudes twice his size. One of them was punching him in the face, and blood gushed from his nose and all over his shirt. Bikini Top snuggled against another dude—obviously her man. A security guard grabbed the bigger dude and pulled him off of Chris, who was yelling profanity. Paul grabbed Chris.

"Let's get out of here," Paul said as he passed me, forcefully pulling Chris along.

I held on to Daria in order to shield her from the drama. Daria, Derrick and I followed Paul as he escorted Chris out the door.

"I'm not ready to go!" Chris yelled, stumbled and tried to force his way back inside of the bar. "I wasn't finished with him."

"Oh yes, you are ready to go," Paul said and pulled him away from the door. "He was definitely finished with you."

"What's wrong with you, man?" Derrick yelled and pushed Chris even though he was already injured. "I'm tired of your crap!"

"She was my girl," Chris slurred, referring to the blonde. "I had her first."

"Obviously not, man," Paul said. "She left with somebody else, dude."

"Why would you bring us here, get pissy drunk and then cause all this chaos?" Derrick was angry and started pushing Chris around. "I can't believe I followed you here!"

"Cut him some slack, man," I told Derrick.

"Don't tell me what to do," he spat back.

"I'm not telling you what to do," I said. "It's already bad…let's not make it worse."

"Let's just go home," Paul said.

"You all right, man?" I asked Chris. "You're holding your ribs like you're hurt. And you can barely walk."

"I'm fine," Chris insisted as he stumbled and fell to the ground. He rested his back against an ATM machine for support. He held on to his side and moaned. He was in pain.

"I think we should find a hospital or something," I suggested.

Paul sighed. "Yeah, you're probably right."

"I'm out of here. I don't have time for Chris and his craziness," Derrick said and then turned toward Daria. "I'm on my way back to campus. I can see that you get there safely."

"That's very sweet," she said. "Thanks. But I'm gonna stay with Marcus."

"Fine. Suit yourself. I'm out of here." Derrick headed for the train station, never looked back.

"Marcus, get us a cab," Paul suggested as he tried to help Chris to his feet.

Daria shivered from the cool night air and I handed her my blazer. She wrapped it around her arms and gave me a warm smile. I was grateful that she hadn't accepted Derrick's offer and decided to stay with me. I flagged down a cab driver who just happened to be creeping along the street. He pulled next to the curb and we all piled in. Daria hopped into the front seat and the three of us in the back. The cabbie rushed through yellow lights as he drove us to the nearest emergency room.

thirteen

Marcus

The emergency waiting room was filled with injured and sick people. A man sat in a chair across the room, his elbows resting on his knees, his hands covering his face. He was in pain, and waiting for his name to be called seemed to take an eternity. There were people who had worse problems than his, like the woman with a bloody gash in her leg and the young boy whose jaw was swollen. He held an ice pack on it, but it didn't seem to help much.

Daria flipped through a magazine while I sipped on a cup of hot chocolate and pretended to watch the television mounted on the wall. Paul was busy sending someone a text message from his phone as the three of us waited for Chris to appear through the double doors that he'd disappeared through earlier. He'd been back there for almost two hours and the waiting was starting to wear on me.

"If you two want to go back, I'll wait here for Chris," Paul finally said.

"Nah, he shouldn't be much longer," I said. "We've been here almost two hours already. It can't be that much longer."

As soon as I said it, Chris walked through the doors. A bandage was on his wrist and he seemed to be holding on to his midsection. He searched the room for familiar faces and Paul and I stood.

"What's up, man?" I asked.

"Fractured ribs." He lifted his shirt and showed us the bandages around his stomach. Then held his arm in the air. "And a broken wrist."

"But you're going to live?" Paul asked.

"Yep," he said. "Let's get out of this stinkin' place. Lots of germs floating around in here, man!"

People gave him cross-eyed looks when he made the germs comment. Nobody ever taught Chris how to be diplomatic or sensitive. He just said whatever came to mind, without regard for the person on the receiving end of his comments. The first day I met him, I wanted to fight him. But the more time I spent with him, the more I felt sorry for him.

We strolled through the automatic doors of the hospital. It was dark outside and it had started to rain. The thunder was loud and lightning flashed across the sky. The rain was relentless.

"We're going to need a cab," Paul said. "I'll go inside and call for one."

He disappeared through the automatic doors and we took a seat on a bench outside.

Chris moaned from the pain. "This is worse than the time my old man threw me out of the house. I mean, literally…threw me out of the house."

He laughed but I knew he didn't really find it funny. He laughed to keep from crying. I looked in his eyes and I saw the history of hurt and pain. I didn't know what had taken place in his life between birth and now, but something wasn't right. And I had a feeling it wasn't his fault.

"Why'd he throw you out?" I asked.

"Because he's a jackass. That's why," is all he said. "And he'll get what he deserves one of these days."

Get what he deserves? What did he deserve? Everything in me wanted to ask that question aloud, but I kept it to myself. Didn't want to get all into his business but I was definitely curious.

He stood, started pacing the sidewalk. Maybe he thought that by pacing he could relieve the pain. He pulled his phone out of his pocket with his good hand, flipped it open, pressed a few buttons and then slammed it shut. Agitated, he took a seat on the bench again.

Paul strolled through the automatic doors, headed our way. "Cabbie should be here in a moment."

Fifteen minutes later, the yellow cab pulled into the circular drive in front of the hospital. Chris climbed into the front passenger's seat as the rest of us piled into the back. The driver was Jamaican, with a red, green and black knitted cap covering his dreadlocks. Reggae music played on his radio and he bounced his head to it.

"You can turn that crap off," Chris said before we were even a block away. "How about some music that we can all listen to and enjoy? Like pop, rock or rhythm and blues?"

Was he serious? I wish I could see his face just to see if he was cracking a smile. It was hard to believe that someone could be that tacky. The driver simply ignored him but that didn't stop his inappropriate comments. "I'm sure you don't understand one word I'm saying." He laughed. "Communication barrier, of course. Would it be too much to ask for you people to stay in your place…in *your* country? You're just as bad as the Hispanics…coming over here illegally… stealing our jobs…bringing that…that…what is it? That swine flu virus crap…"

I couldn't believe my ears. And I wasn't surprised when the cab came to a screeching halt.

"Get out!" the cabbie said.

I peered out the window as the rain pattered against it. I wasn't about to get out of a cab in the middle of a rainstorm.

"Are you serious, dude?" Chris asked.

"As a heart attack," the cabbie said.

"What was it…the music comment?" Chris asked, laughing. "Or was it the swine flu virus comment? I'm sorry, man…."

"All of you…get out of my cab!"

"What did we do, man?" I had to know, because I hadn't said one mumbling word.

The cabdriver refused to respond. He didn't say another word as the four of us piled out of the car one at a time.

"How much do we owe you, sir?" Paul asked, trying to smooth things over.

"Nothing," he responded. "I just want you out of my cab."

As soon as Paul shut the door, the cabdriver peeled away from the curb, leaving us standing there, rain pouring on our heads.

"Thanks a lot, Chris," Daria said; her hair was instantly soaked and she slipped my blazer from her arms and covered her head with it. Tried to stay dry, but it was raining too hard.

"What's with you, man?" I asked.

"Yeah, man. This is certainly not acceptable," Paul said.

Daria, Paul and I started moving toward the nearest train station, and after discovering that the rain wasn't about to ease up, we started jogging at a light pace. It was two blocks to the nearest train station and we left Chris behind. He wasn't able to move as fast, and all of us had silently agreed that we'd had enough of him. He knew his way back to campus. I glanced over my shoulder at him. He was limping slowly down the block, frowning from the pain with every step. Part of me wanted to go back, help him along. I contemplated it for moment, but lost the thought just as quickly.

Kept moving at an even pace until we made it to the train station.

Daria was soaked and I felt sorry for her. Even with wet hair she was still beautiful.

Seated next to her on the "T," I brushed wet hair from her face. "You okay?"

"What a night," she said. "Chris is such a loser."

"He's got some issues. They run deeper than any of us knows," I explained.

"Yeah, you're right, Marcus. He does have issues," Paul added. "And I'm done with him at this juncture. I can't believe we spent the entire night…" he looked at his watch "…and morning for that matter, mucking around with him. First we rescue him from a bar brawl, rush him to the emergency room where we spend hours waiting for him to see a doctor, then we get discarded from a cab in the middle of nowhere…"

"In the rain," Daria added.

"You ever been discarded from a cab, Marcus?" Paul asked, and I had to laugh at his choice of words. *Discarded* from a cab? He made it sound as if we were trash or something.

"Never." I had to laugh just to keep from getting madder.

"I'm embarrassed and humiliated," he said.

For the remainder of the ride back to campus, we were silent. I thought of Chris and hoped he'd find his way back without problems. My body was worn. I needed sleep like yesterday and I didn't even feel like thinking. Leaning my head against the leather seat, I couldn't help thinking about my cozy bed on campus and wanted nothing more than to crawl into it. My phone buzzed and I pulled it out of my pocket. A text message from Indigo.

WUP?

I thought about not answering. What was she doing up at this hour anyway?

I sent a text back. What R U doin up?

Said U wud call after da party...

Things got crazy.

U ok? I'm worried.

I'm ok.

U sure Marcus?

I'm sure...get some z's...Talk 2MORO?

K

Sleep tite. That was my last text before shutting my phone.

Daria was watching me. When I glanced at her, she gave me a smile. She wanted to know who I was texting. I could tell. I stood as the train approached our stop, and when the doors opened automatically, I let her go first. I was happy to be that much closer to home.

As we walked across Harvard Yard, Paul headed toward our dorm and I headed toward Daria's.

"I'm just gonna walk her...make sure she gets in safely," I told him.

"Okay, Marcus. See you later."

We shook hands and Paul headed in the opposite direction. Daria and I strolled toward her dorm.

"You didn't have to walk me the whole way," she said. "I'll be fine."

"Just wanted to make sure."

In front of the building that she called home, we stood under the moonlight. The rain had stopped and Daria handed my blazer to me. It was wet and wrinkled. I threw it over my shoulder and Daria grabbed my hand in hers. Before I knew it, her arms were around my neck, her body pressed against mine.

"Good night, Marcus." She kissed my cheek and then wiped the lipstick from my face with her fingertip.

"Good night, Daria," I said. "Sorry about what happened tonight."

"Not your fault. I enjoyed just being with you, though."

"Same here."

"You got a girlfriend, Marcus?" She asked the question that I was sure had been burning in her mind all through the night.

"Yeah."

"Are you serious about her?"

"Yeah."

A look of disappointment on her face, she removed her arms from around my neck. "Can't blame a girl for trying, right?" she asked.

I didn't respond. I just watched as Daria walked away and headed toward her dorm. If I had the girl of my dreams in College Park, Georgia, then why on earth was I standing here wishing that Daria had kissed my lips instead of my cheek? I didn't have the answer right then, but as I walked toward my dorm, I knew that I had to figure it out.

fourteen

Tameka

The Fourth of July. And the picnic table in the backyard was filled with ribs, chicken, pork chops and hot dogs. A huge bowl of potato salad sat right in the middle of the table, and Jell-O cake with whipped cream on top looked inviting as I made myself a plate. My parents and Uncle Rich and Aunt Annette listened to Frankie Beverly's entire CD and I wondered if they forgot that there were young people there, too—or cared. I thought they should at least mix the music up a little bit—play a little Frankie Beverly and then a little Kanye West—a little Marvin Gaye and then a little Beyoncé. What happened to the compromise?

The Fourth of July used to be one of my favorite holidays—right up there next to Christmas and my birthday. But this year I wasn't quite feeling it. It was hot and muggy in Atlanta and the mosquitoes were eating me alive. And every time one of my little cousins popped a firecracker, I nearly jumped out of my skin. One time I thought my water would break and I snatched the pump from my cousin Nate.

"What did you do that for?" he asked, unaware of the fact that he was getting on my last nerve.

"Because," is all I said.

"Because what, Tameka? I was using that pump!" Nate yelled.

"Not anymore." I smashed the fire out on the sidewalk.

I was always glad to see my twin cousins, Nick and Nate, but only for a short time. I knew it wouldn't be long before they started to run me crazy, and being pregnant didn't help much at all. In the city for less than twenty-four hours, they'd already broken my iPod, drank up all of my favorite juice that was in the refrigerator and destroyed my bedroom. Their Wii had been hooked up to my television since the moment they arrived.

However, I was glad to see their sister, my older cousin Alyssa, despite the fact that her little brothers drove me crazy. I hadn't seen her since my Grandpa Drew's funeral and we had so much to catch up on. She hadn't seen me since my stomach had grown to be the size of a small watermelon and my ankles were swollen. The last time she'd seen me, we had sat huddled in the small bathroom at Grandpa Drew's house awaiting the results of my home pregnancy test. It was the day that my life had changed forever.

"Wow, you are really big," she said as she dropped a heaping spoonful of potato salad onto her plate.

"Thanks a lot."

"I didn't mean it like...an insult or anything." She smiled. "It's just that...your stomach grew so fast...."

"I know, and it's only gonna get worse. I'll get bigger before I get smaller."

"You talked to Vance?" she asked the million dollar question that everybody wanted an answer to.

"Not often. He's so busy with classes and basketball, he doesn't have much time for his pregnant girlfriend." I said it sarcastically.

"Does he know that he's just as much responsible for the baby that his pregnant girlfriend is carrying?"

"He knows," I groaned and took a bite from my pickle. I changed the subject. Everybody seemed to have their opinions about Vance and I really wasn't in the mood for hearing them. "What about your little college boyfriend? He still around?"

It was no secret that Alyssa had been dating an older guy. Much older. He was in college and her parents had no idea about him.

"T.J.?" She smiled and I knew the answer to my question. "I'm gonna have his children someday."

"Not anytime soon, I hope."

"Of course not anytime soon, Tameka. I have to finish college before I even think about getting serious with anyone. I think I'm in love with him, though."

She didn't need to tell me that. Her eyes said it all. It was obvious that she'd already slept with her nineteen-year-old boyfriend who attended FAMU. The evidence was written all over her face.

"I hope you're using protection," I said.

She was shocked by my comment; didn't know what to say, so she simply rolled her eyes.

"I'm serious, Alyssa. Make sure you're using protection. You don't want to end up like me, pregnant at sixteen."

"I'm protecting myself, okay?" she whispered.

"Good," I whispered back.

I took a seat at the table, set my plate down in front of me and began to devour my food. It seemed that the more I ate, the hungrier I became. It was as if my hunger could never be satisfied. Alyssa took a seat across from me at the table. The music seemed louder and Daddy was playing more old school than new. And Indigo and the rest of my friends hadn't shown up yet like they'd promised. They were late.

When I sent Indigo a text message, I found out that they'd had a change of plans. Somehow they ended up at Six Flags instead. At first I was hurt that they hadn't bothered to invite me, but after thinking about it I realized that Six Flags wasn't a place for a pregnant person. I wouldn't be able to ride any of the rides and all the walking would have me worn out and I would've probably spent the entire day sitting on some bench in the middle of the park—watching my friends have the time of their lives. Six Flags definitely wasn't for me.

When I heard a loud giggle coming from the house, I recognized it. Fawn from my exercise class. She waddled from the kitchen carrying a dish covered in aluminum foil. Her son Sean followed behind her carrying a case of soda. He looked handsome in his crisp tan shorts and orange shirt. He wore orange-and-white sneakers to match. I couldn't help noticing that orange definitely looked good against his dark brown skin.

"Who's that?" Alyssa asked. "He is fine."

"His mama is in my prenatal exercise class."

I watched as Mommy introduced Fawn and Sean to Daddy. She took the dish from Fawn and set it on the table with the rest of the food. Daddy took the case of soda from Sean and placed the cans one by one into the cooler. When Mommy started looking around the yard, I knew she was looking for me, and once she spotted me, they all headed my way.

"There she is," Fawn said as she approached. "Here's our little mommy."

I stood and gave her a hug.

"What's up, Tameka?" Sean said in his deep voice.

"What's up, Sean?" I said, "This is my cousin, Alyssa. Alyssa, this is Fawn from my exercise class and this is her son, Sean."

"Hi." Alyssa smiled at both of them.

"Nice to meet you," Fawn said and shook my cousin's hand.

Sean simply gave her a nod that said "what's up?"

Fawn disappeared into the house with my mother; the two of them running their mouths and catching each other up on the latest gossip. Sean made himself a hefty plate filled with ribs, chicken and potato salad and took a seat at the table next to me. As the wind blew, I caught a smell of his cologne. It was an enticing smell, made me want to lean closer just to inhale it.

"What was that dish covered in foil that your mama brought?" I asked. It seemed that food was the most interesting thing in my life these days.

"It's just some peach cobbler that she made this morning," he said.

"Are you for real?" I asked. Just the thought of it lingered in my mind for a few moments.

"Yeah. My mom makes the best peach cobbler." He smiled. "You should try it."

"I plan to."

"You want me to get you some?" he asked.

"You would do that?"

"Of course," he said and stood. "You stay right here. I'll be right back."

Alyssa stared at me. Her hand on her chin, a goofy grin on her face.

"What?" I asked.

"He likes you," she said.

Her comment was ludicrous. No one as fine as him would be interested in someone as pregnant as me. Not when there were thousands of unpregnant pretty girls in the Atlanta metro area. Not to mention, even if he did *like* me as Alyssa seemed to think, I had a boyfriend. There was no hope for any type of future for us. Vance and I were still a couple. He was just away at school, just for a moment. He would be back during the holidays and we would be a family just as soon as the baby was born. There was no room for anyone else in my life.

"He's just being nice," I said, and couldn't help sneaking a glance over at the food table to watch as he made me a plate of peach cobbler.

"He's cute, though, isn't he?" Alyssa smiled as she stuffed a forkful of potato salad into her mouth.

"He is cute. I give him that, but I do have a boyfriend," I said.

"When's the last time you talked to this boyfriend anyway?" she asked.

"Last night," I told her. "He said that he was driving down to Mississippi with a few friends from school to spend the Fourth of July."

"Do you think he's excited about the baby?" She asked the one question that I'd asked myself a million times. Sometimes I wondered if he even remembered that there was a baby growing inside of me.

"Of course he is," I told her, and hoped that I was right. "He's just a little scared. But so am I. We can't let that get in the way of our future, though."

Sean walked up and placed the peach cobbler on the table in front of me.

"Here you go." He smiled.

I watched as he took a seat at the table and began to dig into his food. He was a sweet guy, I thought. He'd be a perfect match for one of my girlfriends. I just had to figure out which one.

fifteen

Vance

The drive from Grambling to Jackson seemed to take forever as Jaylen and I sat cramped in the backseat of Jessie's Kia Sportage. Mississippi's heat was muggy—worse than Atlanta's heat in July. And it didn't help that Jessie's air-conditioning didn't work. Lexi drove the entire way, the two of them in the front seat running their mouths the whole time. I was glad when she finally pulled the car into the driveway of a huge two-story house. The house was white with black shutters on all of the windows and sat on a huge piece of land. I was willing to bet that it was more than an acre.

The four of us stepped out of the car and followed Lexi up to the house. A huge barbecue pit was fired up next to the porch and some older dude was flipping burgers, ribs and chicken on it. A group of people were playing horseshoes and laughter filled the air. Another group of young men tossed a football back and forth to each other, and there was a card table set up on the opposite side of the yard where four people played Bid Whiz and cussed each other out.

A full-figured woman with a face that was identical to Lexi's stepped out the front door and onto the porch as we approached.

"Hi, baby." She grabbed Lexi and hugged her tightly. "I was expecting you last night."

"We decided to drive down after practice this morning," Lexi explained and then changed the subject. "Mama, these are my friends…this is Jessie. She plays on the team with me. And these are my friends Vance and Jaylen."

"So nice to meet you all," Lexi's mom said. "I'm Katherine Bishop. You can call me Kat. Everybody does. I know y'all are hungry. Come on in here and get yourselves something to eat."

We followed Kat through the immaculate living room with plastic still on the antique-looking furniture. The hardwood floors were shining so bright you could almost see your reflection in them. In the kitchen, there was so much food that you could barely see the countertops. Several large pans of food were covered in aluminum foil.

"Grab yourselves a paper plate and dig in," Kat said. "Lexi, you know where everything is. Make sure you take good care of your guests."

Kat disappeared and the four of us grabbed plates and began to load food onto them. I wasn't wasting any time. I was hungry and Lexi's mother had instantly made me feel at home with her Southern hospitality. I sat next to Lexi at the island in the kitchen and stuffed my face with barbecue ribs. I didn't care that there was sauce all over my face, and I didn't even mind when Lexi took the corner of her napkin and wiped it off.

After dinner, Jaylen and I played horseshoes with Lexi's father, Don Bishop, and her three uncles. It was my first time playing the game, but it wasn't rocket science and I caught on pretty quickly. That didn't make it any easier to compete against men who were experts at the sport. They whipped our pants off and then sent us into the house to play a game that they claimed was more our speed—Bid Whiz—with Lexi's aunts.

"Come on in here, babies, and sit down," Lexi's aunt Florence said as we looked on.

"We'll teach you how to play," her aunt Doris said.

"She'll teach you how to cheat," Aunt Florence corrected her. "Because that's all Doris ever does is cheat."

"I don't cheat. I'm just an expert at the game."

Jaylen and I sat across from each other at the card table, pretending we knew what we were doing. Aunt Florence and Aunt Doris taught us everything they knew, and for a brief moment we were actually giving them a run for their money—their quarters anyway. We were playing for quarters and by the end of the night I had lost every one that I had in my pocket. I was sure that Jaylen was broke, too. We knew it was time to get up.

After a few games of Bid Whiz, Jaylen and I joined Lexi and Jessie in the family room where they were watching *All About The Benjamins,* a movie that I'd seen at least ten times. But I sat down to watch it again for the eleventh time. I plopped down onto the leather sofa next to Lexi, where she snuggled close to me—so close that I could smell the oils that she'd just bathed in. Jaylen sat in a chair in the corner of the room and Jessie sat with her legs crossed on the floor. Lexi and Jessie had both showered and changed into pajamas.

We watched *All About The Benjamins* and then Lexi popped in *Friday After Next,* and we laughed about everything that Day-Day had to say. Just the look on his face was enough to make us laugh. I couldn't remember the number of times that Jaylen and I had watched all the *Friday* movies. We knew each line word for word, and no matter how many times we'd watched it was always just as funny as the first time. After the credits from the movie rolled up the screen, I started to feel tired.

"You think I can grab a shower?" I asked Lexi.

"Of course. Let me show you where you and Jaylen will be sleeping tonight. There's a bathroom attached to your room."

I followed Lexi down the long hallway; my sneakers made a squishing noise in the plush carpet as I tried to tiptoe, careful not to wake her parents. After ushering everyone out of the house, they had said their good-nights and then retired to their bedroom. But not before her father gave us all strict instructions about our sleeping arrangements and warned us that there would be no funny business.

He looked me square in the eyes when he said, "If everyone obeys the rules, then I won't have to break nobody's legs."

His shoulders were broad like a bodybuilder's. His head was bald and his beard was graying. He didn't seem like anyone that I wanted to be in a confrontation with. I had every intention of obeying his rules and keeping my legs intact. After all, it was his house and I was too far away from home to be playing with my life.

Lexi stopped in front of a room with blue walls and two twin beds against each wall, with a nightstand in between them. The blue-and-red plaid comforters made the room feel manly and I was glad there weren't a bunch of flowers everywhere. It seemed warm and comfortable.

"Here we are." She smiled. "You and Jaylen can sleep in here. Let me grab you a towel and a washcloth so you can take a shower."

"Cool," I said. I took a seat on one of the beds and watched as Lexi disappeared down the hallway.

"Who are you?" A young boy wearing a Celtics jersey popped his head into the room.

"I'm Vance. Who are you?"

"Zach," he said. "Are you my cousin or something?"

"Nah, I'm Lexi's friend," I said.

"Do my parents know that you're here?" he asked right before Lexi pushed him out of the way.

"Get out of the way, big head," Lexi said and pushed Zach inside the door before I could respond to his question. She explained, "This is my little brother, Zachery. He's a ten-year-old nosy busybody. And don't pay attention to anything he says."

"We met," I told her.

"Shouldn't you be in bed?" Lexi asked Zach.

"Shouldn't you be in bed?" Zach asked her, a grin on his face. "Does Mama and Daddy know that you have a boy in the house?"

"Yes, they know." Lexi sighed. "Now can you please go away?"

"I'm gonna go ask 'em," Zach threatened.

"Go ask!" Lexi said. "And take your big head to bed while you're at it."

Zachery left the room, but not before popping Lexi on her behind—hard.

"Ooh, I can't stand little brothers! You don't have one, do you?" she asked.

"No, but I got a little sister. And she's just as annoying. Maybe even a little worse." I smiled.

"Nah, nobody's worse than him," Lexi said. "Here's your towel and washcloth. The bathroom is right through there." She pointed toward a doorway that was attached to the room.

"Cool, thanks." I grabbed them and headed for the bathroom.

"Hey, Vance," she said before leaving, "my room is right down the hall." She smiled a sly little smile. "Jessie's sleeping in the guest room upstairs and I'll be all…alone. Maybe you can come visit me later."

"But your daddy said…"

"Forget about him. He's all bark and no bite," she said. "My room will be the one with the SpongeBob SquarePants purse hanging on the door handle. I'll leave it there just for you."

It was no secret that Lexi loved SpongeBob SquarePants. She was wearing the character's pajamas and slippers. And one time on campus, I caught her wearing a SpongeBob T-shirt.

"Okay, I'll think about it," I told her, but I wasn't sure if I was going to chance it. I grabbed a pair of underwear from my overnight bag, headed for the bathroom and turned on the shower.

When I stepped back into the bedroom after my shower, Jaylen was already reclined on the twin bed across from mine, his arms resting behind his head and his legs crossed.

"Man, this crib is dope." He smiled. "I could get used to this."

"Yeah, it is pretty nice," I said, standing there with a towel wrapped around my waist. "I think I'm gonna go check on Lexi. See if she's asleep yet. Maybe tuck her in; read her a bedtime story."

"Yeah, right." Jaylen smiled. "You creeping into her room, ain't you?"

"I'm just going to check on her." I smiled back. "But don't wait up."

We both laughed as I gently pulled the door open and stepped out into the hallway. I walked softly down the carpeted hallway in search of Lexi's purse that she said would be hanging on her door. I spotted it and crept up to the door, turned the knob and quietly pushed the door open. It was dark inside and I wondered why she hadn't left the light on for me, especially since she was expecting me. After all, she had invited me. For what, I wasn't sure. We hadn't been intimate yet. The most we'd done was kiss, although the chemistry was definitely there. I guess curiosity had brought me down this long hallway, just to see what Lexi had in mind.

"Lexi," I whispered. It seemed that she was already in bed; I could see the lump underneath the covers. "Lexi, you sleep?"

Suddenly the light from the bedside lamp nearly blinded me.

"Young man, why are you in our bedroom calling for Lexi?" Kat sat straight up in bed.

"Why are you looking for Lexi in the first place?" Mr. Bishop asked, a crease in the center of his forehead. "And wearing nothing but a bath towel?"

"Um…" I didn't really have an answer. I was shocked and embarrassed and knew that my life was possibly in danger. My heart was beating at a rapid pace.

"Didn't you hear me tell you earlier that I would break both of your legs, son?" he said. "I wasn't playing with you."

"Be nice, sweetie." Kat patted her husband's hairy chest, which was more than I wanted to see.

"Go put some clothes on, son, and meet me in the kitchen," he said. "I want to have a word with you."

My heart pounding out of control, I turned to walk away. Strolled slowly through the Bishops' bedroom door and back down the hallway. What was Lexi thinking? Was she trying to set me up or what? Didn't she know that her father was scary? It was then that I spotted her little brother standing in the dark shadows of the hallway, his arms folded across his chest, a wicked smirk on his face.

"Looking for someone?" He giggled.

"You little…" I lunged toward him and he took off running. I wasn't about to chase after him in a house I knew nothing about. I let him go but promised myself that I would get him later. He wasn't about to get away with setting me up, I thought as I stepped quietly into the guest room.

"That was fast," Jaylen said. "She obviously wasn't giving up the booty."

"Man, I busted in on Lexi's parents. It wasn't even her room."

"Word?" Jaylen laughed. "How did that happen?"

"Her little brother playing games. He switched the purse on the door handle…" I tried to explain everything to Jaylen but from the look on his face, I could tell that he had no idea what I was talking about. "Anyway, Mr. Bishop wants to talk to me…in the kitchen."

"Now?"

"Right now."

"Ooh, for real?" Jaylen asked and placed his fist over his mouth. "Dog…you in trouble. I'll start packing our things while you're gone. That way we can go ahead and get an early start on our walk back to campus. Maybe we could even hitchhike…."

"Jaylen, shut up." I slipped on a pair of jeans and pulled a wifebeater over my head, then reluctantly walked down the hall toward the kitchen. It seemed to be the longest walk of my life as I made my way to the kitchen. Mr. Bishop sat at the kitchen table waiting patiently for me to arrive. At that point, I knew that my days were limited.

sixteen

Tameka

A game of Monopoly was always a good way of finding out about somebody's business sense. It was a game where you got to feel grown-up and make decisions about paying bills and buying property. Sometimes you ended up broke and disgusted while the person across the board from you was rolling in the dough and laughing every time you landed on a piece of their property. That person tonight was Sean. He owned every piece of high-dollar property there was on the board—Boardwalk and Park Place, Pacific, North Carolina and Pennsylvania Avenues. Alyssa and I were afraid to even approach his side of the board for fear that the next time around we might actually be homeless.

"Feel free to give up at anytime," Sean said boastfully. "I own just about everything on the board so I'm just gonna continue to take all of your money."

"Not a chance!" Alyssa said as she rolled the die.

She was a competitor by nature. She was an athlete and loved a challenge, even when she was losing. She never gave up, no matter what. When we were little and played board games or even a simple game of hopscotch, it always turned into a serious competition for her. Even when she lost, she wanted a rematch. Sometimes when I refused to give her a chance at beating me, she would pout and stop speaking to me for a couple of hours.

For me, it wasn't that serious. As I landed on Boardwalk one last time, several little red hotels posted up along the board, I knew that it was over for me. I handed over my last few dollars to Sean.

"I guess I'm out of the game," I announced. "I'm officially broke."

"I didn't mean to take your money like that." Sean smiled and then looked over at Alyssa, who wasn't smiling at all. "You give up, too? I'm kind of tired of whipping y'all."

"No, boo. I still have money left." She counted her last few green and pink dollars. "Plus I'm about to get two hundred dollars for passing Go."

"That's if you make it there." He started rubbing the hairs on his chin.

"Just give up now, girl," I told her. "There's no way you're making it past Boardwalk."

She rolled the die and then advanced nine spaces. As she landed on Park Place, she rolled her eyes at Sean. "I want a rematch," she said.

"Nah, I don't feel like playing another game. It's too long," he said and stood. "I think I'm gonna head outside and check out some of the fireworks. You coming, Tameka?"

"Cool. Yeah," I said and tried to lift myself up from the living room floor. When Sean saw me struggling, he offered a hand. He pulled me up and I lost my balance and fell into his arms.

"You okay?" he asked.

"Yeah, thanks," I said and then followed him toward the front door. "You coming, Lyssa?" I asked.

"Nah, I'm gonna go help Aunt Mel put the food away and clean up in the kitchen," she said. "You kids have fun."

I rolled my eyes at her and then followed Sean out the door and into our driveway where my little cousins were popping firecrackers. Sean and I found a couple of lawn chairs in the garage and placed them in the driveway next to each other. It was a beautiful night as I looked up into the sky and checked out the moon and stars. I wondered if Vance was looking at the same moon and stars, and wondered if he was thinking of me at that moment. It was a romantic scene, I thought, as I took a seat next to Sean.

"The moon is pretty cool, huh?" he asked. "It's like God placed it there just to smile down on us."

"You think so?"

"Aw yeah. Look at it...how beautiful it is," he said. "It's almost as beautiful as your smile. I meant to tell you that earlier...that I like your smile."

"Thank you." I couldn't help blushing. It wasn't often that guys paid me compliments. Teenage boys were usually focused on other things like...themselves. And when they paid compliments, it was usually about your body parts— your butt, your breasts, your legs. Never your smile.

"So...is your boyfriend helping you out...you know, with the pregnancy and stuff?"

"Well, since he's away at school, his parents send me money to help out with buying the things that I'll need for the baby...like clothes and a car seat. His mom gave me a crib that used to belong to Vance. He slept in it when he was a baby. I thought that was sweet," I said and realized that I was rambling. I couldn't remember if I'd answered Sean's question, so I simply said, "I'm hoping that she's born during Thanksgiving while Vance is home on break."

"That would be cool," Sean said. "So you already know it's a girl?"

"Yeah, I had a sonogram done a few months ago and

found out that it was girl. But I didn't tell Vance yet. I wanted it to be a surprise."

"Do you love him?"

"Of course. We're gonna get married after we both finish college."

"I hope he's not like the dude that got my mother pregnant. He didn't stick around that long at all—didn't even step up to his responsibilities. And for that, I lost respect for him. I thought he was a pretty cool dude until then. Now I just wanna hit him in his jaw."

"Yeah, that was pretty lame," I said, remembering the story that Fawn told the group on the first night we met. "Vance denied our baby at first…telling me that it wasn't his. I think guys are probably scared at first, until the reality of it sinks in. And then they come around. Maybe Fawn's ex will come around, too."

"Maybe. But it's too late in my opinion. He put her through too much hurt. I've listened to her cry too many nights over this. He can't ever step up on my doorstep. I'm the man of that house and I won't allow it. I've been with her through thick and thin…going to her doctor's appointments and her exercise classes."

"I know what you mean," I said. "I would be so mad at him."

"So your boyfriend finally came around…started claiming the baby?"

"Yeah, he came around and decided to step up to the plate. He was scared at first, because he thought his future was down the drain. But he finally saw that he could still go to college and everything and still handle his responsibilities, too."

"That's good," he said. "My cousin goes to Grambling State. He's down there taking some summer classes. I thought of going there myself but changed my mind. I wouldn't be

STEP UP 113

able to focus down there…lots of partying going on. So many frat parties and girls…lots of girls. I saw pictures of the girls that are down there. They are hot! I would be kicked out before my second semester."

His comment about frat parties and girls caused my heart to pound. I wondered if Vance was down there partying and having fun with other girls at my expense. His phone calls *had* become less frequent and when I was able to catch him on the phone, he was always in a hurry to end the conversation. He claimed that he was busy with basketball practice and summer classes. And the reason he didn't call so much was because he had to be careful about using his phone. His parents had warned him about roaming fees since he was out of state. He said that college was way different than high school and that it required more time and focus. The last thing I wanted to do was place unnecessary pressure on him while he was down there trying to make a better future for me and our baby. So I let it go. I knew that he loved me and that was all that mattered at the moment. But listening to Sean talk about what he'd heard about Grambling raised concerns that I hadn't had before.

"So, they party a lot down there?"

"Yeah. Every weekend there's a frat party or something going on," he said. "I'll probably go down there for a weekend visit soon. My cousin wants me to come and check out the campus, even though I already know I'm not going there. I've already been accepted to Georgia State."

"You don't seem excited about it," I said.

"It's cool. Whatever makes my moms happy, you know? She deserves more than I can really give her right now, but it's just the little things that count. She was all excited about me getting accepted into college. She didn't even care which one, just as long as I was going. Nobody in our family ever went to college before."

"Same here. That's why I have to go, for everybody who didn't," I told Sean.

"Your moms is cool," he said. "She seems so young and hot. Was she mad when you got pregnant?"

"She wasn't really mad, just disappointed because she wanted better things for me. Now she just drives me crazy about things like what I eat and how I dress. She's so over-protective. And I know it's only gonna get worse after the baby's here."

"She's just looking out...like good moms do." He smiled and stood. "You wanna take a walk?"

"Okay," I said and stood, too.

We headed out of my driveway and down the block. Where? I wasn't sure, but I was enjoying the conversation we were having; I didn't want it to end. Sean was easy to talk to and very easy on the eyes. The sound of fireworks going off echoed throughout the city. There was a cloud of smoke in the sky left behind from the bottle rockets, firecrackers and M-80s that people were lighting up every two seconds. Even though fireworks were illegal in the state of Georgia, people managed to still find them and shoot them regardless. Daddy always made the short drive to Chattanooga just to buy the illegal goods and smuggle them across the Georgia state line. Everybody did it, and nobody ever got arrested for shooting the fireworks. I often wondered why they made rules that they didn't bother to enforce.

Sean grabbed my hand as we strolled down the block. I didn't even mind. In fact, it seemed natural as I compared my hand to his. His were so much bigger, and nearly swallowed mine. They were softer than most boys' hands. We turned the corner and spied on some boys shooting hoops on the next block. Someone else was barbecuing right there in their driveway. A few houses down, an older couple sat on their porch and probably gossiped about everyone who walked past. And finally, the nerdy guy who lived on the corner polished his red sports car and stared as we walked past. The Fourth of July seemed to bring everyone out of the house for one reason or another.

"What does it mean when your boyfriend is away at college, and you barely hear from him…he hardly ever calls, and when you call him…he's always in a hurry to get off the phone?" I asked Sean.

He shrugged. "I don't know. It could mean a lot of things. It could mean that he's busy. It could mean that he's partying and having a good time…."

"Could it mean that he's messing around with some-body else?"

He shrugged again. "Put it like this…if you're really into somebody, you would make time for them no matter what. Especially somebody who's carrying your baby. I know if I had a girl like you at home while I was away at college, I would be calling her every day just to check on her…make sure she was okay."

"You're sweet." I smiled.

"And you're beautiful," Sean said.

"Thank you for hanging out with me today," I told him.

"No problem. Anytime," he said. "Let's head back to the house. I don't want your mother thinking that I kidnapped you." As we walked back toward my house, I felt happier than I had in days. Worrying about what Vance was doing while away at college was a full-time job…and an exhaust-ing one. And I was too young to be worried or exhausted.

seventeen

Vance

Mr. Bishop waited patiently for me at the kitchen table, a look of disgust on his face.

"Have a seat, son," he said and motioned for me to take the seat across the table from him.

"Yes, sir," I said nervously. "I'm sorry about the misunderstanding earlier. I was just coming in to say good-night to Lexi and…"

"Forget about it, son," he said. "Talk to me about your future. I know that you're attending that university down there in Louisiana on a basketball scholarship, but what is it that you're studying? You know that basketball will only take you so far. You got to have some other things under your belt. Do you have a plan?"

"I'm planning to go to law school, sir. My mother is a lawyer and I want to follow in her footsteps."

"That's a good career choice. Lots of money to be made, although most of the lawyers I know are liars and cheaters…but hey, everybody can't be honest."

I didn't know what to say about that comment, so I didn't say anything. My mother was a lawyer and she wasn't a liar or a cheater. I just kept quiet and listened as he rambled on about his lying lawyer friends.

"You ain't got no kids, do you?" he asked.

I hesitated for a moment. I wasn't ready to admit that I had a baby on the way, especially since I hadn't even told Lexi. "No, sir, I don't."

Technically it wasn't a lie, since…at the moment, I *didn't* have any kids. The baby wasn't born yet, so therefore I wasn't anybody's father—just yet. Not to mention, the longer I stayed away from Georgia, the less true it seemed. I'd found the reality easier to cope with since I was in another state. In another state I could be who or whatever I wanted to be. I could recreate myself and no one would ever know. If I decided that I didn't really have a baby on the way, then it wasn't true. If I decided that I didn't have a girlfriend waiting for me back home, then it wasn't true. So tonight, it wasn't true.

"That's good, son," Mr. Bishop said matter-of-factly. "Kids nowadays are having kids left and right and they're too doggone young to be parents, in my opinion…."

I was silent. Didn't agree. Didn't disagree.

"Just so you know, my daughter has hopes and dreams for a bright future. She intends to finish college and have a successful career before she even thinks about having children. Furthermore, she will be married first. She can't afford to be careless," he said, and I knew where this conversation was going. "Mistakes can't be reversed. You understand what I'm saying to you, son?"

"Yes, sir," I said.

"Good. I'm glad we have an understanding. Now I want you to go into that guest room and get yourself a good night's sleep. And in the morning, I want you and your friend out of my house."

"Okay."

He stood, tightened the belt on his robe.

"Good night, son."

"Good night, Mr. Bishop."

He headed down the hallway. I stood slowly; dropped my head. I was embarrassed. Not to mention I felt guilty about lying to Lexi's father. It hurt to know that I was that dude that he was protecting his daughter from. I was that person who was too young to already have his girlfriend pregnant in Atlanta. I felt ashamed. Wished I could go back to that night; change it. Even though Tameka and I had been careful, we were still living with the consequences of our actions. And for that we would pay for the rest of our lives.

Lying there in the guest bedroom, staring at the ceiling, I thought about my future. I knew that dating a girl like Lexi was out of my reach. She didn't need a guy like me in her life. She deserved someone whose future didn't include changing diapers and warming formula on top of a hot stove. And Tameka deserved a better boyfriend than the one I had been to her. I had been treating her badly and acting as if she didn't even exist. As long as I didn't have to look at her huge stomach and listen to her stories about swollen ankles and being tired all the time, then her pregnancy wasn't real to me. I could do whatever I wanted to do. Nobody in Grambling, Louisiana, knew that I was a father-to-be. But as I lay there, I knew that I needed to change all that. Tameka deserved more, and my plan was to call and let her know just as soon as I got back on campus.

The next morning, I wasn't interested in the country breakfast that Kat had laid out for us—scrambled eggs, sausage, hash browns, fluffy pancakes, grits and orange juice. It looked good, but I'd lost my appetite after last night's fiasco. I wanted to get back to campus as soon as possible. Unfortunately I had to wait for Lexi, Jessie and Jaylen to scarf down as much food as their stomachs could hold before we finally piled into Jessie's car. I was quiet on the drive back to campus as Jessie and Lexi ran their mouths the entire way. Every now and then Jaylen would jump into the conversation. But as far as I was concerned, I had too much on my mind for small talk. Mr. Bishop had definitely given me some things to think about.

When we pulled into the school's parking lot, I hopped out of the car, grabbed my bag from the back of the car, told everyone goodbye and headed toward my dorm. Lexi hopped out and rushed to catch up to me.

"Wait up, Vance," she said. "Aren't you gonna walk me to my dorm?"

"I'm kind of tired. Just trying to get to my room and relax a little bit. Got class tomorrow. I just need a little space. Is that cool?" I didn't give her a chance to respond before I said, "I'll call you later."

"Okay," she said. "Are you hungry? Because you didn't eat anything for breakfast. You want me to go grab you something?"

"Nah, I'm all right. Not hungry."

"And you don't want any company?"

"Just wanna be alone for a while."

"I'm sorry about what my little brother, Zach, did. He can be so stupid sometimes. You forgive me?"

"It's not you, Lexi...or Zach or anything like that. I just need some space, okay?"

"All right," she said reluctantly. "Call me when you feel like talking."

She turned to walk away and then began to jog toward her building. Her feelings were hurt but I couldn't worry about that. I had other things on my mind and I needed to be left alone.

Once inside my dormitory, I collapsed onto my bed. Eyes staring at the ceiling, I tossed a basketball into the air. Jaylen walked in and dropped his gym bag onto the floor.

"What's up with you, man? I'm really starting to worry about you. You didn't say two words all the way home." He placed the back of his hand on to my forehead. "Are you sick?"

"Just got a lot on my head, man. I'm seventeen and about to become a father. And I didn't really realize how huge that was until my conversation last night with Mr. Bishop."

"You told Lexi's father about the baby?"

"Of course not," I said. "But it was almost like he knew...like he could see through me or something."

"Did he threaten to kill you?"

"Just to break my legs." We both laughed.

"What's on your mind then?"

"I gotta make things right with Tameka. I have to step up to the plate and do the right thing by her."

"Well, you know it's a frat party going on tonight. Can you make things right with her in the morning...*after the party?*"

I knew that the right thing to do was say no. I had no business thinking about a party when I had other worries going on. But curiosity had me in a headlock and wouldn't let go. I felt guilty about wanting to know the details of the party, but asked anyway, "Who's throwing it?"

"The twins, Sheila and Sherry. Those two beautiful vanilla-colored girls with the voluptuous...um..." He made a motion with his hands like he was cupping a set of breasts. "Where you been? That's all we talked about on the drive home. Weren't you listening?"

"Not at all. My mind was somewhere else."

"Well, we have to go. At least show our faces." He grinned. "There will be girls, girls and more girls. You know that, right?"

I nodded a yes.

"Cool. Then we're going, right?"

"Can't miss it," I said.

"I'm hitting the showers then." He pulled his T-shirt over his head and then headed toward the showers.

I sat on the edge of my bed—wondered if my Boston Celtics jersey was clean because I had plans for it. Whatever I was feeling at Lexi's parents' house and on the way home was slowly fading away. It wasn't anything that a hot party couldn't fix.

As loud music rang in my ears, soft, skinny arms wrapped themselves around me from behind. A sweet voice whispered in my ear, "Hey, Vance."

I turned to find a set of pretty brown eyes looking square into mine. The cute little dimple doing a dance on her cheek. I hadn't seen Shay since Jaylen and I first stepped on campus; since the day that she and her girlfriend, Kim, had invited us to a party. I had hopes of seeing her at the party that night, but there were so many people there. Looking for her would've been like looking for a needle in a haystack.

"What's up, girl?" I took a glance around the room just to make sure that Lexi wasn't somewhere watching as some girl wrapped her arms around me. Lexi and I weren't officially committed but I liked her. Didn't want her feelings to be hurt over someone I barely knew.

"Nothing's up. Where you been hiding?" she asked. "I've been hoping to bump into you somewhere."

"Well, you haven't been looking very hard. I play ball, remember?"

"That's true," she said.

When the deejay slowed the music down, we both started rocking to the music.

"You wanna dance?" I asked her. It seemed only natural to ask her to dance, considering we were both swaying already and the song was nice.

"Yeah," she said and followed me to the dance floor.

My arms around her waist and hers around my neck, we talked about meaningless things like school and whether or not I was adjusting to college life. It was hard to focus when her cologne was intoxicating me; it made me want to pull her closer but I remained a gentleman. When the conversation changed to a more personal one, I knew that Shay was interested in a lot more than dancing.

"Truthfully, I've been watching you practice just about every day, Vance. Hoping that you would notice me up there in the stands checking out your game," she admitted.

"I didn't know you were up there." I blushed. "Why didn't you holler at me or something?"

"Because I'm not used to hollering at guys. I'm used to guys hollering at me," she said.

"But if you see something you're interested in, why wouldn't you let somebody know?" I asked.

"I don't know. I guess I'm letting you know now...that I'm interested. What you got to say about that?" she asked.

"I say...that's nice," I said.

"A friend of mine has an apartment not far from here. It's empty tonight. I can take you there and show you just how interested I am."

"Um..." I took a glance around the room again, in search of those beautiful eyes that belonged to Lexi. She was nowhere to be found and a pretty girl wanted to show me how interested she was in me. "Okay. You got a car?"

"We don't really need a car...that is, if you don't mind walking."

"I can walk."

"Cool. Let's go."

On the way toward the door, I spotted Jaylen who had already started a conversation with Shay's friend, Kim. They were sipping from cups filled with something when I approached. Shay pulled Kim aside and obviously ran our plans down to her. I leaned in closer to Jaylen, just to give him an update as well.

Before I knew it, I was strolling down a dark unpaved road, headed for whatever adventure the night had in store for me.

eighteen

Marcus

I sat in the common area of our dorm suite, iPod in hand and earbuds inside of my ears. My African American studies book open, I tried to focus while taking notes. The television was tuned to the news as Jae ferociously took notes in a spiral notebook, Paul listened intently to the newscaster on television, Chris argued loudly with someone on his cell phone and Derrick played a game on his PSP.

He looked up at me. "So what's up with the girl, Marcus? Daria?" he asked.

I shrugged. "I don't know, man."

"I thought you were gonna hook me up." His eyes were steady on his game. "What happened to that?"

"What made you think that Marcus was going to hook you up with her? It's obvious he wants her for himself." Paul smiled.

"Marcus can't be interested in her," Chris said. "He has a girlfriend in…what's the name of that city in the middle of Atlanta's ghetto, Marcus?"

"Is he talking to me?" I asked, offended that he was referring to my neighborhood as the ghetto.

"Marcus is from College Park, Georgia," Paul interjected.

"Yeah," Chris said. "That's where his girlfriend lives."

"Marcus's girlfriend, Indigo, is very beautiful," Jae said. "I saw her picture."

"How would she feel if she knew you were running around campus with another girl, Marcus?" Chris asked. "Better yet, how would you feel if she hooked up with someone else back there in…College Park?"

"First of all, me and Daria are just friends."

"Marcus, it's Daria and I." Paul corrected my bad English.

"Yeah, Daria and I are just friends. Not that it's any of your business anyway," I said to Chris. "And secondly, I trust my girl and she trusts me."

"I think the more appropriate question is do you trust yourself?" Chris asked.

As anal as Chris was, and no matter how inappropriate his conversation was, the truth was he had a point. I didn't trust myself around Daria. And I didn't trust myself when I wasn't around her. She always seemed to find her way into my thoughts in the middle of the day. Sometimes I wondered what she was doing there and occasionally I could even smell her perfume in my head. It had only been two nights since her beautiful face had last crept into my dreams and already I missed her.

The whole thing was confusing. I didn't know how to explain what I was feeling. I loved Indigo, missed her smile and longed to hold her in my arms. We sent text messages back and forth all through the day and sent photos of each other with our camera phones. We talked each other to sleep every night and she woke me up every morning with her bright, sunshiny voice. Indigo was the girl of my dreams. Wasn't she?

Hooking Daria up with Derrick should've been easy for me, but it wasn't. I didn't want to. He wasn't good enough for her—not like me. I was a much better choice, and even though I was taken, I didn't want to see her with anyone else. I wanted her to myself. And the truth was she wanted me.

I flipped open my phone and sent her a text.

Hey U. WUP?

U. Daria responded.

What U doin 2nite?

Waitin 4 U to take me to the coffee house.

Now? I asked.

The thought of seeing Daria again made my heart race. Part of me wanted to get to her before Derrick. Although his chances with her were slim to none, I wanted to make sure he never made it to first base. If I had to spend every waking hour with her, just to make sure, then that's what I intended to do.

Yes now, Daria replied.

On my way. I typed the words without hesitation—without rethinking my plans of staying in for the night...studying for my exam.

Before I knew it those plans had changed and I was closing my book. I stood up and headed for my room. I changed shirts, sprayed a little cologne on my neck and brushed my waves. I slipped my Jordans on to my feet and popped a mint into my mouth. As I strolled through the living area and reached for the door, all eyes were on me.

"I'm just gonna step out for a little bit," I explained to the guys.

"Where you going, Marcus?" Paul asked.

"Out for coffee," I said and before anyone could ask another question, I was already shutting the door behind me. I didn't feel like explaining or being judged by anyone. I didn't feel like hearing Chris's mouth about my girlfriend in the ghetto, and I definitely didn't want Derrick tagging along just so he could catch a glimpse at the best-looking girl in Boston. What they didn't know wouldn't hurt them.

Daria looked good in her tangerine-colored top and jeans that hugged every curve of her hips. She gave me a hug, her head resting against my chest. She grabbed me by the hand and pulled me in the opposite direction of the "T" station.

"Thought we were going to the coffeehouse," I said.

"I wanna show you something first," she said.

We approached the entrance of a nearby park, her hand holding on to mine tightly. Daria leaned against the trunk of a tree. Before I could think about it, I was leaned against her and our lips were locked instantly. Not like the kiss at the bar, which was more soft and friendly—a brotherly kiss. This one was more of an I-want-you-right-now type of kiss. I wrapped my arms tighter around her small waist; I pulled her closer.

"What am I doing?" I asked myself, not realizing that I'd said it aloud.

"You're kissing me." Daria smiled. "Are you nervous, Marcus?"

"Not really nervous, but…"

"But you're thinking about your girlfriend? Wondering what she would think about you kissing another girl?"

"It's wrong."

"She's not here, and what she doesn't know won't hurt her."

She had a point. Indigo was miles away and unless I told her about kissing Daria, she wouldn't know. Still, I felt guilt in the pit of my stomach; kind of like the feeling I got that time when I failed American History and couldn't think of the words to tell my parents. I knew they'd be disappointed.

Indigo believed in me and trusted me to do the right thing. Just like I trusted her to keep her lips off of another dude, she expected the same thing from me. And here I was betraying her. Suddenly, kissing Daria didn't feel so good.

"I don't want to hurt my girl, Daria. I mean, you're beautiful and interesting…and…you know, you have a lot to offer. But I love my girl."

"I understand, Marcus. But when you think about it, she's so far away. And before long, you'll be going away to college for good. In less than a year, you'll be a freshmen here at Harvard and she'll be…what? Still in high school?" she asked. "Will your relationship with her survive Harvard, Marcus?"

That was a question that I'd never thought about. It was true. I would be leaving Georgia soon…for good—not just for the summer. I'd be a college student soon and Indigo would still be walking the halls of Carver High School, dancing on the school's dance team and doing other things that high school girls did. She would be so far away that I wouldn't see her very often. Not to mention we would have less in common. I wouldn't be able to have intellectual conversations with Indigo—about world history and the state of our economy, like the debates we had in class. She wouldn't understand things like that. Being at Harvard over the summer had me thinking different—about important things like my future and how Indigo wasn't really on my level anymore. She was still a kid. Daria, on the other hand, was more mature—a woman. She understood things and we had more in common. We were both Harvard students who could hold intellectual conversations with each other. It was no secret, I liked her.

"Come here. Let me show you something." Daria grabbed my hand.

I followed her as we climbed a steep hill. At the top, we took seats side by side on the green grass underneath an oak tree that overlooked the entire city. It was a nice view—like something out of a magazine or in a movie. It was one of the views that you wanted to take a picture of and place in a photo album. Daria got closer and grabbed my hand in hers.

"It's nice up here," I said.

"Romantic, huh?"

"I guess you could say that."

We sat there for at least an hour, talking about things. I told her all about Indigo and she talked about the boyfriend that she had left behind before going away to college. She told me about her family and the fact that her parents got divorced the summer before she went away to school. She was still bitter with them about it. I totally understood how she felt because I'd felt the same way when my parents were divorced. It was like my life had stood still.

Daria told me about a guy that she'd gone on a date with in her first year at Harvard. He was aggressive and wanted to have sex with her on the first date. When she said no, he'd grabbed her by the arm and shoved her into the wall. Tried to force himself on her. Luckily she was able to break free and took off running. When she got to her dorm, she told her roommate about what happened but never told anyone else. Never pressed charges. Never even brought it up again until now.

"Why didn't you tell someone in authority?" I asked her. "That was date rape!"

"Well, since he didn't really get that far, I just let it go."

"Does he still go to Harvard?" I asked. "Do you still see him around?"

"Yes," she said and seemed uncomfortable about talking about it all of a sudden. "I see him all the time. Now can we talk about something else?"

"Okay." I said it but didn't really mean it. I wanted to finish our conversation about the date. I wanted to know who he was and confront him about it. I wondered if it was too late to bring charges against him.

"You seem like the perfect gentleman, Marcus. Like you wouldn't hurt a fly." She smiled. "Indigo is a lucky girl."

"Yeah, she is pretty lucky." I laughed. "So let me ask you something...why won't you give my boy, Derrick, some play? He's feeling you."

"He's not my type," she said matter-of-factly.

"What is your type?" I asked.

Before I knew it, her lips were against mine again. I knew I should've pried them away but I couldn't.

"You're my type, Marcus," she whispered.

I knew I needed to get back to reality but I wasn't sure how. I was trapped between what I wanted to do and what I knew to be the right thing to do. The right thing to do was to get up and run back to my dorm as fast as I could. But I was paralyzed. Indigo's face was in my head but Daria was in my arms.

nineteen

Tameka

SIPPING on peach-mango-flavored smoothies, we listened to the quiet storm on V-103. As Lauryn Hill's "Ex-Factor" rang through the speakers, six girls pretended they knew the words. It was more of an old-school song and I only knew some of the words because Mommy had played it over and over a million times when I was little. We all danced around the patio as the music rang out across our backyard. It felt as if I'd never left the dance team as I moved my hips and belly to the music.

Asia and Jade stopped and took sips from their smoothies while Indigo and I did the bump. Tymia and my cousin Alyssa giggled as they watched. Alyssa wasn't really much of a dancer; she was an athlete, but she enjoyed hanging out with us anyway. We had talked her parents into letting her stay in Atlanta for a few weeks. They'd left for Florida the day after the Fourth of July holiday and planned on coming back for Alyssa at the end of the month. We were both shocked and excited but didn't ask any questions. We were just glad for the time together. With us living so far apart, it wasn't often that we got to spend time together.

I couldn't wait to introduce her to my friends and just as

I suspected, everybody hit it off immediately. Once Alyssa and Tymia discovered that they were both in love with Omarion—*this week*—they became the best of friends right away. Asia was a little standoffish at first, but that was just her. She did that with everyone until she got to know them. After she warmed up a little, she and Alyssa actually had a discussion about fashion that lasted way too long in my opinion. Indigo and Jade wanted to teach her the latest dance steps even though she wasn't at all interested in learning.

"See what's playing on 95.5 The Beat," Jade suggested. "The quiet storm is kind of lame. I don't know any of those songs. Who the heck is DeBarge anyway?"

"I know who DeBarge is. My mama used to listen to them back in the day," said Alyssa.

"That's my point," Jade added.

I switched stations and Young Jeezy's and Kanye's voices echoed across the dark sky.

"Now that's what I'm talking about right there." Indigo shook her booty to the music and then pulled Tymia out of her lawn chair. "Show me that move that you did in practice the other day."

"This one?" Tymia bounced her shoulders and moved her hips to the music.

"Yeah, that's it…slow it down a little bit so I can get it," Indigo said.

Tymia repeated the move slowly and we all lined up along the patio and tried to mimic it. Before long, we all were moving in unison. Even Alyssa had it. We all spent the next hour showing each other dance moves. The best part about being a teenager was having sleepovers like this one and having all of your friends in one place at one time.

"Are y'all still at it out here?" Mommy slid the glass patio door open and stuck her head out. "Is anybody hungry?"

"No, thank you, Mel," Indigo answered for the group. "We're cool."

"Thanks, Mommy, but we're good," I added.

"Okay, then. I made some quesadillas in case y'all get hungry later. Tameka, they're in the oven and..."

Mommy was interrupted by loud screams as Lil Wayne's "Lollipop" began to play. All of us started shaking to the music as if he was making an appearance in our backyard. Discovering that she'd lost our attention, Mommy quietly shut the patio door and disappeared inside. She knew from past sleepovers that my friends and I would stay up until the wee hours of the morning dancing, singing and talking about everything under the sun. She always made sure that the kitchen was stocked with our favorite drinks and snacks and never complained about the giggles and loud conversations.

After the mosquitoes started to bite, we took our party inside to the family room where we spread blankets on the floor and flipped through the channels. The radio was still playing quietly although we watched television. When UGK's and Outkast's "Walk It Out" song started to play, Jade didn't hesitate to turn up the volume while Tymia and Indigo started to Walk It Out. Asia and Jade couldn't help joining in, and it wasn't long before Alyssa and I started Walking It Out, too. Walking It Out didn't come so easy for me anymore—not with my stomach protruding across the room. Still, I moved to the music. The exercise was good for me *and* the baby.

Jamie Foxx's "Blame It" rang out across the room, my ringtone. I rushed to grab it, hoping it was Vance. It had been two days since I'd heard from him and I needed to hear his voice. I looked at the screen; it was a number that I didn't recognize but I answered anyway.

"Hello," I said it cautiously.

"Tameka, what's up?"

"Who's this?" I asked.

"It's me, Sean."

"Hey, what's up?" I said. I was disappointed that it wasn't Vance but glad to hear Sean's voice. "Whose number is this?"

"This is my cousin's phone. My battery went dead," he explained. "What you doing?"

"Hanging out with my girls."

"Sounds like y'all are having a party."

"I guess we kinda are," I explained.

"What's the occasion?'

"None. We're just having a sleepover, hanging out...listening to some music, you know, the usual."

"That's cool," he said. "Hey, check this out...I'm going down to Grambling in a few days to hang out with a couple of my friends on campus."

"Really?"

"Yeah, I'll probably leave on Thursday and come back Sunday. You want me to check some things out while I'm there?"

"Like what?" I was playing dumb. I knew exactly what he wanted to check out.

"I could check up on your boyfriend—make sure he's behaving himself." Sean laughed, but I wasn't laughing. Insecurity had already begun to set in and my trust in Vance was slowly fading away with each passing day. However, I still loved him. And I wanted to believe in him.

"Nah, I'm good," I told Sean.

"Well, if you change your mind, let me know. I got your back," he said.

"I appreciate it. Thanks."

"Well, I'll let you get back to your party. Wish I was there." I could hear the smile in his voice.

"It's just a bunch of giggling girls over here. You would

be bored." I smiled and took a seat on the sofa; curled my feet underneath my bottom as I got comfortable.

"I wouldn't be bored if I were with you," he said. "Your beautiful smile would keep me company."

I giggled as if Sean had told a joke. He made me smile for no apparent reason at all and when I finally looked up, every eye in the room was on me. They were all wondering who I was talking to.

"Tell Vance I said hello," Indigo said.

"Indigo said hi," I told Sean…pretended he was Vance.

"Tell her I said what's up." He played along. "Matter of fact, ask her if I can come over."

"Tonight?" I asked. The idea of it was exciting.

"Right now," he said. "I'll bring some friends to meet your friends. What'd you say?"

"I guess it would be okay. My mom is sleeping…so…okay." I said it before I clearly thought it through.

"Cool. I'll see you in a minute then."

I hung up and sat there for a minute, gathered my thoughts. Knew that I needed to do something with my hair, maybe put on some lip gloss. There was no way of hiding my stomach. A bigger shirt would only make me look bigger. And why did I care anyway? Sean knew that I was pregnant. And he was just a friend anyway.

"That wasn't Vance, was it?" Alyssa asked.

I shook my head no, a sly grin on my face.

"Who was it then?" Indigo asked.

"Yeah, 'cause you were all smiles and everything," Jade added.

"It was Sean, wasn't it?" Alyssa asked.

"Who's Sean?" Asia asked.

"Sean from the exercise class?" Indigo asked. "I knew he liked you!"

"Like her?" Alyssa asked. "He's been over here kicking it with her."

"He's been over here?" Indigo asked. "And you didn't tell me? You been holding out on me!"

"Okay...okay...he came over on the Fourth of July," I explained. "And he's on his way over now."

"Right now?" Alyssa asked.

"Are you for real?" Tymia asked.

"And he's bringing some friends," I told them.

"Are they cute?" Jade asked.

"I don't know. He's cute, so his friends probably are, too."

"Oh my God! When were you gonna tell us?" Asia grabbed her purse and rushed into the guest bathroom. "I gotta comb my hair and put on some lip gloss."

"Asia, let me borrow your eyeliner pencil," Tymia said and went into the bathroom, too.

Indigo, Jade, Alyssa and I crept up the stairs and crowded into the other bathroom, careful not to wake Mommy. I checked my hair in the mirror and put on lip gloss. Indigo did something with Jade's hair while Alyssa sat on the edge of the bathtub and sent a text to someone. Probably her college-aged boyfriend. When "Blame It" echoed through the small bathroom, I grabbed my phone quickly. Didn't want Mommy to hear it.

"Hello," I whispered.

"Come outside," Sean insisted.

"Okay," I said before hanging up. I turned to my friends. "They're outside."

We made a beeline for my bedroom just so we could peek out the window and try to catch a glimpse of Sean and his friends before going downstairs. As they stood underneath the streetlight in front our house, we could tell that there were four of them...Sean and three other boys. One of them wore cornrows in his hair. With his sagging jeans, his muscles were defined against his tight-fitting T-shirt. Another boy had a short haircut and had dark skin and big eyes. He wore shorts and a wifebeater. His friend sported a Coogi outfit and brushed his waves.

"Okay, they're cute...from what I can tell," Jade said.

"I got the Omar Epps look-alike," Asia smiled.

"You are so fast," Indigo exclaimed. "Don't nobody want him."

"Whatever, Indi." Asia laughed.

"How about the tall, dark and handsome one in the denim shorts and Lakers jersey?" Jade asked.

"That's the one that belongs to Ta-me-ka," Alyssa said.

"He doesn't belong to me. He's just a friend," I corrected her. "Now let's go before they wake up my neighbors."

Standing on the curb, we all talked and laughed about nothing in particular. Asia and Omar Epps stepped away and began a private conversation of their own. Tymia laughed as Cornrows whispered something into her ear and Jade started quizzing the boy in the Coogi outfit about the rap industry. Alyssa, Indigo and I gathered around Sean to get a better look at his CD collection.

"I got anything you wanna hear," he bragged. "Old school, new school, rap, R & B. You name it."

Holding T.I.'s CD in her hand, Indigo said, "I would marry him if I wasn't already hopelessly in love with Marcus Carter." Her eyes became dreamy. She missed Marcus way more than she let on.

"Is that your boyfriend?" Alyssa asked.

"Yep...always and forever." Indigo twirled the charm on her necklace, the other half of a silver heart that she shared with Marcus. He wore the other half around his neck.

I always envied Indigo and Marcus's relationship from the day they got together. Marcus seemed like the perfect boyfriend and I believed that other boys could learn a thing or two from him about how to treat a girl. Marcus was Indigo's knight in shining armor.

"My boyfriend is sweet, too. We're getting married after we both graduate from college," Alyssa announced.

"He's already got a head start on you, girl," I teased. "What is he...like a junior in college?"

"Tameka, don't get me started on your missing-in-action boyfriend, Vance," she fired back, and although her words were accurate, they still hurt. I dropped my head as a slight pain shot through my heart. "Sorry." Alyssa grabbed my arm and placed her head on my shoulder. "I shouldn't have said that."

"What *is* up with Vance?" Indigo asked. "He really needs to do better."

"I told her that I could check up on him if she wanted me to. I'm headed down to Grambling for a weekend stay." Sean smiled. "I could rough him up a little bit."

"And I said that it's not necessary," I interjected.

"When are you leaving?" Indigo asked, and I could see the wheels in her head turning.

"Thursday morning. Me and my buddy Calvin over there is driving down there in his Jeep."

"And how much room is in this...Jeep?" Indigo continued.

"What are you thinking, Indi?" I asked skeptically.

"Got plenty of room. It's just the two of us," Sean said. "Why? Y'all wanna roll with us?"

"No," I said.

"Come on, Tameka. You know you wanna go down there and see what Vance is up to. Besides, it would be fun...something to do...a chance to get away for a few days."

"I agree. It might be fun," Alyssa added.

"Our parents will never agree to it," I reminded both Alyssa and Indigo. Indigo could barely spend the night at my house without the third degree. I wasn't sure how she figured she'd get them to let her go to Louisiana for the weekend.

"I could tell my parents that I'm spending the weekend at your house and you could tell Mel that you're spending the weekend with me." Indigo began to plead her case. "It's doable and you know it."

"I don't like lying to my mama," I said.

"Then tell her the truth," Alyssa suggested. "Aunt Mel is really cool. She's nothing like the rest of our parents."

"Tell you what...y'all figure it out and let me know," Sean said.

I secretly found the idea very interesting but didn't want any of them to know just how much. I would give anything to get down to Grambling and see what Vance was doing. I would surprise him and he would be so happy to see me. It would be a reunion that would give me pleasant dreams for months to come.

"We'll let you know," I told Sean.

"Let him know about what?" Jade was all up in the business all of a sudden; her newfound friend, who happened to be Sean's friend, Calvin, was standing close by.

"We're thinking about going down to Grambling with Sean on Thursday," Indigo explained.

"That's it. We're just thinking about it," I stressed.

"I wanna go." Asia approached and joined the conversation, too.

"Me, too." Tymia came out of nowhere.

"Why don't we all go," Calvin suggested. "I can probably get my dad's Suburban. It seats nine people and as long as y'all don't pack too much stuff we could probably do it."

"Yeah, you know how girls get carried away with all the shoes and clothes and stuff," Sean said.

"The gas will probably kill me, but it'll be worth it to hang out with Jade a little bit." He gave Jade a smile.

"I didn't say I was going," Jade teased. She was all smiles, too. Whatever she and Calvin were talking about earlier had her blushing, and it was obvious that they liked each other.

"You should consider going. That way we could get to know each other a little better." Calvin didn't have to do much convincing before she agreed.

"Okay," she said.

It seemed that the conversation had gone from "we'll think about it" to "what time we getting picked up on Thursday" and nobody had even considered what we were going to tell our parents. I could barely sleep that night as thoughts of Vance raced through my head. Seeing him was long overdue. As I mentally picked out the outfits and shoes I would pack, I knew that Thursday would take its time coming around.

twenty

Vance

with my size-eleven Jordans spread across the floral comforter, the lights dimmed and the scent of some sweet-smelling candle floating through the air, I wrapped Shay in my arms. Kissing her was like sucking on a peppermint because she had just popped one into her mouth. My hormones raged out of control as her head rested in the center of my chest. As music played softly on the stereo, I shut my eyes and wondered where the night would take us. I knew that sleeping with a girl had its consequences, especially since I was already dealing with a pregnant girlfriend in Atlanta.

In addition to my relationship with Tameka, I had a girl on campus that I was starting to fall for, too. She was definitely my type...athletic, smart, had a sense of humor...everything I wanted in a girl. Tameka represented what was right while Lexi represented what felt good. And now here I was adding to the equation. Shay was beautiful and sexy. She wasn't quite the type of girl I would take home and introduce to my mother. She was known around campus as hot and easy to get into bed, especially if you were an athlete. She was one of the groupies who hung around the gymnasium hoping that one of the basketball players would show just a little bit of interest in her. In my mind, she was simply a quick toss between the sheets.

She lifted my arms and pulled my shirt over my head and began planting soft kisses all over my chest. My self-control was slowly fading away as I lifted her shirt over her head. Her brown breasts were plump beneath her pink bra. Her stomach was flat and sexy with a silver navel ring glistening in the darkness. She removed her skintight jeans and dropped them to the floor. I did the same, but not before searching my pockets for a condom. I searched in each pocket thoroughly and couldn't find one. I pulled out my wallet and checked the compartments, too. Nothing.

"I don't have a condom," I announced. "You got one?"

"No, Vance. We don't really need one. Just go with it."

"Nah, I don't roll like that. Gotta use protection."

"I don't have no STDs or anything. I'm clean."

"I believe you, but before I lay with someone I gotta protect myself." I sat up in the bed. The mood was different. As much as I wanted Shay, I knew that it was stupid to move forward.

I stood, slipped my jeans back on.

"What're you doing?" she asked. She seemed to become angry.

"Hey, baby, as much as I want this right now, we can't afford to be careless. There are too many diseases out there…"

"Diseases? You think I got a disease?" She was standing, too, with her hands on her hips. Her pink underwear was looking all cute in the moonlight that crept into the window.

"I'm not saying you got a disease. I'm saying that I don't get down unless I got some protection. And you shouldn't be sleeping with anybody unless they do the same. You feel me?"

"Yeah, I feel you, Vance. You're just a tease is all you are. Brought me all the way over here for nothing!"

She was scaring me; made me want to take off running as far away from her as possible. But I played it cool. "Sorry you feel that way, Shay," I told her, grabbed my shirt from the floor and headed for the front door. She ran after me and pushed me from behind. When she began to yell all sorts of obscenities, I knew it was definitely time to go.

Before I approached the door, a key was stuck into the lock from the other side and the front door swung open. A group of at least five giggling girls rushed into the apartment. The leader, a light brown girl with short curly locks, looked me square in the eyes.

"Who are you?" she asked.

"I'm, uh…" It was as if I'd forgotten my name as a familiar, angry pair of eyes popped up from behind Curly Locks and looked right into mine.

"His name is Vance," Lexi said as she pushed her way into the apartment. She gave Shay, who was standing behind me, a look of disapproval as Shay stood there in her pink underwear.

"Shay, what's going on up in here? I didn't say you could use my apartment to get your little freak on. You said that you wanted to come here and study because you can't concentrate in your dorm room," Curly Locks stated.

I didn't wait around to hear Shay's response to her friend. I was too busy running after Lexi who had bolted out the door and down the stairs. I thought I saw tears in her eyes before she ran, and my heart ached. I never meant to hurt her. In fact, I couldn't even figure out why I was in some strange girl's apartment, with a girl that I knew was easy, about to make one of the biggest mistakes of my life.

"Lexi," I called out to her.

Her friendship meant more to me than a roll between the sheets with Shay, and I felt as if I'd lost it. She stopped running but started strolling at a fast pace.

"What do you want, Vance? You got everything you need right up them stairs…standing there in her little pink panties waiting for you!" She turned just long enough to say that.

This was a side of Lexi that I'd never seen before—angry. She had daggers in her eyes and was not at all interested in talking to me. She kept walking but I caught up with her.

"I don't care about that girl, Lexi…I was just…"

"Just what, Vance? You was just trying to get between her legs?"

"It wasn't even like that…" I grabbed her hand, only to have her yank it away.

"Then what was it like?" Her eyes were softer now and they were staring into mine. It was better when they were angry because the softer eyes made me feel guiltier. My heart started to ache as she waited for an answer to her question. "What was it like then?"

"Okay…it was like that. I did try to sleep with Shay. But I didn't."

"Why didn't you?"

"Because…" I looked away, suddenly ashamed. I felt worse than I had in a long time. Hurting Lexi was bad. It hurt me inside. "Because I didn't have any protection."

At least I was honest. She had to give me credit for that.

"That's the only reason you didn't sleep with her?"

"Um…yeah." The truth was all that I could give her. If she wanted more, then that's all I had. After all, I was a young man with raging hormones. And Shay was beautiful and sexy. Anyone with eyes could see that. The guys on the team had bragged about bedding her; they talked about how good she was and I wanted to see for myself. Wanted to see what all the hype was. "It ain't like we're committed or anything…you and me. I thought we were just kicking it."

"I guess that's what it is then. We're just kicking it."

"Yeah, 'cause you got that dude back in Mississippi…what's his name?"

"Tyrone," she whispered, "and I don't want him. If I wanted him, I wouldn't have been hanging out with you."

"I'm sorry. I wasn't trying to hurt you, Lexi. What were you doing over here anyway?"

"The girl that lives there, Andrea, is one of my best friends. She's on the basketball team. We hang out at her place all the time. Nobody felt like partying tonight, so we were headed over to her apartment to watch some movies and maybe order some pizza. You said that you needed some space, wanted to be alone, remember? I didn't expect to find you there with…Shay Taylor…one of the biggest hoochies on campus. I knew that everyone else slept with her but I thought you were different."

I wanted to believe that I was different but the truth was, I wasn't. I didn't have a response for Lexi. I didn't know what to say.

"You and me…we just friends, right?" I asked.

"I thought we were more than friends, Vance. I thought you were feeling me, like I was feeling you."

"I am feeling you, but we never really talked about it like that."

"You mean like a commitment or something?"

"Yeah, we never made any commitments or anything."

"So that's why you thought it was okay to sleep with Shay? Because we didn't have an official commitment?"

"Something like that." I said it but wished I hadn't. The truth of the matter was I couldn't really commit to Lexi. I already had a commitment with someone else.

"So let's make a commitment then, Vance. Right here…right now," she suggested, those soft brown eyes piercing me, causing my heart to bleed. I wished I had the guts to tell her the truth. She deserved at least that.

"Right now?" I asked.

"Right now," she repeated.

"I, um…I can't…"

"Fine, Vance. Go sleep with whomever you want." She turned to walk away.

I let her get a few steps away before I stopped her. "Okay, Lexi…you want a commitment?"

She stopped in midstride and turned to face me. "Yes. Right here, right now. I want a commitment. I wanna be the only girl that you kick it with."

"You're already the only girl that I kick it with. Why do we have to get hung up with formalities?"

"Why can't you commit, Vance?" she asked.

"I can." I blew air from my lips. "Shoot, a commitment is nothing to me."

"Then fine. Ask me to be your girl." Her hands were on her hips and I knew she was serious. I knew that I would lose in this situation either way it went. The heart of the matter was, I really liked her and I was terrified of losing her. I had to make a choice, and fast because she was waiting for a proposal.

"Aiight, Lexi. Um…" I could feel the sweat popping out on my forehead. "Will you be my girl?"

"You for real, Vance?" she asked. Why was she asking me if I was for real when she'd practically just twisted my arm?

"Of course I'm for real. Be my girl. And hurry up before I change my mind." Suddenly I was cocky.

"Shut up, boy. You are so silly." She was all smiles then. That sad look was gone and the life was back in her eyes again. She wrapped her arms around my neck, kissed my lips. "That means that you can't be getting your freak on with nobody but me."

"I don't care nothing about that girl back there."

"Not just her, Vance. I'm talking about all girls. You are officially removed from the players' list."

"Okay…so what other rules you got?" I asked.

"I wanna tell my parents. I want to let them know that we are in a relationship."

"That's cool. Maybe your father won't break my legs now." I laughed.

"I'll make sure Daddy behaves. He's just looking out for his baby girl."

"It doesn't really matter. It's not like I'm gonna see your father that often. Probably won't see him again until next Fourth of July."

"Actually, no…you'll see him on Thursday."

"What?"

"Yeah, my parents will be here on Thursday. They're coming down to spend the weekend with me. They want to have dinner with me on Thursday night and I want you to come along."

"I don't know about that, Lexi…I…"

"You have to, Vance. If we're in a committed relationship, then you need to get used to my parents being around. You have to come."

She was persistent and when she gave me that look, I couldn't resist. I didn't know how to say no.

"Aiight, what time?"

"Around six," she said. "Relax, Vance. It's not that serious."

"Right." That's all I could say. Thursday was just a few days away and already I was feeling trapped—like a fly stuck in a spider's web. No options, no way out and slowly dying. I didn't know what the upcoming weekend had in store for me and I wasn't very anxious to find out.

twenty-one

Marcus

I stood in the middle of the floor in my dorm room, a pair of basketball shorts hanging from my hips, a wife-beater hugging my chest, my cell phone in my hand as I stared at the screen. I couldn't believe the phone call I'd just received. It was surreal—like a bad dream. No…actually it was more like a nightmare. Indigo was angrier than she'd ever been before and I couldn't get a word in. She'd used so much profanity I wanted to wash her mouth out with soap.

"You're a lying, cheating dog, Marcus!" she'd yelled.

"What are you talking about?" I had asked as my heart started to pound out of control. I was already on edge from being awakened from a deep sleep. At two o'clock in the morning, I knew that the jingle from my cell phone couldn't possibly be a good thing. I knew something was wrong when I saw Indigo's name flashing across the screen. And when I'd missed the first call, she'd called right back. She would've called back-to-back until I answered.

"You know exactly what I'm talking about, Marcus Carter. I got the photos by e-mail," she growled.

"What photos?"

"The photos of you and…and…that hoochie! You kissed

her, Marcus. And held her." Her voice shook like she might cry at any moment. She was hurting.

My heart beat faster than a normal pace.

"Who are you talking about?"

"Don't play dumb. You down there at Harvard messing around on me? You're supposed to be down there going to school and you all up in somebody else's arms."

How did she know these things?

"Who sent you photos?"

"I got them by e-mail...from...I don't know! From someone who calls themselves Hollywood."

Hollywood...Hollywood...I didn't know anyone who called themselves Hollywood, I thought as I held the phone up to my ear.

"Somebody's messing with you," I explained to Indi.

"So you're telling me that you weren't kissing another girl?"

"Well...um...I did meet someone, Indi."

The dead silence made me think that she'd hung up. That is until I heard the light whimpers in my ear. She was crying and my heart ached. I never meant to hurt Indigo. I wasn't even sure about what I wanted to do—if I wanted to break things off with her because I'd matured over the summer or if I wanted to hold on to her for dear life. After all, we'd been through a lot together. Indigo and I had history. I'd only known Daria for a few weeks and even though I was feeling her, I wasn't sure if she could take Indigo's place. Someone had made that decision for me by sending photos to Indigo's e-mail box. Who would do such a thing?

"Who is she, Marcus?"

"Her name is Daria." I wanted to be honest with her. I loved Indi.

"And she goes to Harvard?"

"Yes."

"She in the summer program, too?"

"Nah, she's a freshman here. She's taking some summer classes. Next year she'll be a sophomore."

"An older woman." She laughed sarcastically. "You like her, Marcus?"

"Yeah, she's cool."

"I can't believe I've been running around here telling people that you're my knight in shining armor. Your armor is faded and rusty. And you're no knight, Marcus. You're no better than Quincy Rawlins, with his trifling behind. And I never want to see you again."

When I tried to respond to Indigo's final comment, I realized I was talking to a dial tone. And so I stood there, holding on to my cell phone, staring at the screen as if she might call back. When I tried calling her, she let it ring; she wouldn't pick up. Whoever Hollywood was, he or *she* was making my life a living hell.

twenty-two

Tameka

Tymia's house was the perfect place to meet since her mother went to work at the crack of dawn. And because her mom, Rita, worked and traveled a lot with her job, none of the rest of our parents had really spent much time with her. My mom met her once at one of our games. Indigo's parents met her at open house at the beginning of last school year. Asia's parents had never met her and Jade's parents met her briefly one time when they dropped Jade off after dance team practice. Nobody had Rita's phone number and none of the parents really knew where Tymia and her mom lived. They just knew that they lived somewhere in College Park. Rita was a woman of mystery who provided all of us with the perfect alibi.

Calvin pulled up in front of Tymia's house in his father's Suburban. He was on time—ten o'clock sharp just like he'd promised. He didn't have to honk; he barely had time to put the gear shift in park before we all burst through the door, our overnight bags in tow, our faces made up in various shades of eye shadow and lip gloss. We all shared the same fragrance as we'd passed the bottle around until each of us had sprayed it on. At least we didn't have five different fragrances going on. Our male escorts might've asked us to walk to Grambling.

Calvin and Sean stepped out; being the gentlemen that they are, they grabbed each of our bags and strategically placed them in the back of the SUV. They'd warned us about packing too much unnecessary stuff and we were careful not to get carried away. I was the shoe queen and usually packed a different pair of shoes for each day when I traveled, but being pregnant had forced me to pack more sensibly. All I needed was a pair of flip-flops to match each outfit and flip-flops didn't take up that much room in a suitcase.

All of us piled into the back of the vehicle one by one. Indigo squeezed in next to me and propped a pillow against the back of the seat. Sometime during the night, she'd slipped outside to Tymia's backyard to talk to Marcus on the phone. When she came back inside, it looked as if she'd been crying. She didn't know that I was watching her as she pulled her hair back into a ponytail and curled up into her sleeping bag on the floor and stared at the ceiling most of the night. I wanted to ask her what was wrong, but it was already late and I knew that we had an early morning. Besides, I didn't want to wake the rest of the girls, who were all scattered around the room in sleeping bags on Tymia's bedroom floor.

Indigo rested her head against the pillow and started to doze almost immediately. I gazed out the window as Calvin maneuvered the SUV through Tymia's subdivision. Tymia and Alyssa started with the chitter-chatter and giggling about nothing in particular as Jade grumbled because they'd stuck her in the middle. Asia sat on the other side of Indigo and started sending someone text messages from her phone. Calvin and Sean bounced to the sound of Jeezy as his voice flowed through the speakers.

I rested my head against the window and thought about

Vance. Wondered what he was doing at the moment. It took everything in me not to text him and let him know that I was coming. I wanted it to be a surprise. I couldn't wait to see the look on his face when he saw me. I'd gained at least fifteen pounds since he'd left. My belly was bigger, ankles were more swollen and my face was fatter. My hair had grown by leaps and bounds and my nails were absolutely beautiful—not that he would care. I smiled as I flipped my phone open and took a long look at his face on my screen. I placed his photo there so that I could see his cute face every time I made a phone call. He was my boo, after all. And I needed him to hold me like nobody's business.

As we approached Birmingham, Alabama, Calvin took an exit off the highway and pulled into the nearest gas station. As the SUV came to a halt, Indigo woke up and checked her mouth for drool. I needed to use the restroom in a major way. I pulled a compact out of my purse and checked my hair before stepping out of the car.

"I need to go, too," Indigo said.

As I waddled toward the restrooms, I wrapped my arm around Indigo's neck. "What's wrong with you, boo boo?" I asked.

"Marcus is cheating." She didn't hesitate to tell me what was going on.

"What? Not Marcus Carter. You must be talking about another Marcus."

"No, I'm talking about Marcus Carter. Somebody e-mailed me some pictures of him with this girl...and...he was kissing her."

"Are you for real?"

"Yes."

"Did you ask him about it?"

"He admitted it."

"Wow, Indi, that's messed up. Who is she?"

"Somebody who goes to Harvard. He likes her."

"I don't believe it."

"Believe it, Tameka. It's true. It's over between us. I told him to lose my number."

"Please, girl, Marcus loves him some Indigo Summer. It ain't over yet. It won't be long before he comes to his senses. Realize that she ain't got nothing on you!"

"She's very pretty." Tears began to fill her eyes.

"Don't cry, Indi. Marcus will come around." I tried to think of something better to say, but there were no words that would make my friend feel better. "He loves you, girl. I know he does. He's just tripping right now."

I liked Marcus and hoped that what Indigo said wasn't true. She believed in him. We all believed in him. He was the type of guy that we all wanted our boyfriends to act like. Every girl who knew Marcus wanted a Marcus in their lives. It was disappointing to think that he might not be the person we held to high standards. There was a chance that he might just be like all the other guys in the world.

Indi pushed the door to the ladies' restroom open and disappeared into an empty stall. I could still hear her sniffles as I locked the door to my stall.

"Who would send you photos like that anyways?" I asked her.

"I don't know. Obviously somebody who doesn't like Marcus very much. The e-mail was from somebody named Hollywood."

Standing at the sink, Indigo wiped tears from her bloodshot eyes.

"Cheer up, Indi," I told her. "We're on our way to Grambling, Louisiana. Maybe you'll have the time of your life and forget all about this stuff…at least for the weekend. I know it's easier said than done, but just try and have a good time."

"I'll try," she said.

"Cool. Now dry your eyes and try to get the red out. We don't want everybody all up in your business."

She wiped her eyes one last time, put a few eyedrops into them. "Thanks, Tameka, for being my friend."

"That's what I'm here for. We're friends 'til the end, right?" I asked her. "And if we need to make a trip up there to Cambridge, Massachusetts, we can do that. We'll turn Harvard out."

"You silly." She laughed.

"I know," I said and then followed Indigo out of the restroom.

I browsed through the store, grabbed a bottle of soda, a package of sunflower seeds and some candy. Placed them onto the counter. I glanced over at Indigo who was aimlessly browsing the candy aisle. She was lost without Marcus. The boy who was once the center of her existence was caught kissing another girl. I felt sorry for her. I wished I could make things better, but some things were just out of my control. All I could do was be her friend, listen when she needed to talk and offer a shoulder when she needed to cry. She grabbed a package of licorice and headed my way.

We were just a few hours from Grambling and I wondered if she would last through the weekend without having a nervous breakdown.

twenty-three

Vance

I took a long, deep breath as I pulled my polo shirt over my head and tucked it into my slacks. I brushed my hair and sprayed some cologne on. It wasn't often that I dressed this way, only when we traveled for away games or the rare times when I attended church. But I wanted to make a good impression on Lexi's father, Mr. Bishop—a much better impression than the one I'd made before. Bursting up into their bedroom wearing nothing more than a towel was not the image I wanted to leave them with. I wanted them to see me for the young man that I was—a college student with a promising basketball career, son of a doctor and lawyer, future district attorney...they needed to see that young man. They thought I was a thug from the hood with nothing on my mind but sleeping with their daughter and that couldn't have been further from the truth.

The truth was I had never even touched Lexi that way. She was way too special for me to simply jump into bed with. I liked her—she was one of the coolest girls I'd met in a long time. I enjoyed being around her, and each night before I went to sleep I couldn't help thinking about her. When she wasn't around, I missed her like crazy. On the other hand, I had Tameka in Atlanta—the mother of my unborn child. I wanted to do the right thing by her. After all, I was just as much responsible for our current dilemma. Besides her plump belly, I liked Tameka and didn't want to see her hurt. She deserved much more than that.

As I sat on the edge of the bed and slipped my feet into a pair of shoes, my phone buzzed. Lexi.

"Where you at?"

"On my way down," I told her.

I took a peek out the window and saw her father's car parked at the curb. The motor revved as smoke crept out the back tailpipe. He sat tall and straight at the wheel, a cell phone pressed against his ear, while Lexi talked to her mother from the backseat.

I slid into the leather backseat and strapped my seat belt on.

"How are you today, Mr. Bishop…Mrs. Bishop?" I asked immediately. "It's nice to see you both again."

"So nice to see you, too, Vance." Kat smiled warmly.

"Vance, didn't Lexi remind you that we had six o'clock dinner reservations?"

"Um…yes, sir. I'm sorry for being late. My basketball practice ran over a little bit," I explained while his deep, dark eyes stared at me from the rearview mirror.

Lexi grabbed my hand with her cold ones and held on to it. She gave me a warm, encouraging smile. Even though the air-conditioning was on full blast, I needed some air and wanted to roll down my window. Anxiety was getting the best of me as I hoped this night would end sooner than later.

Pulling into the hotel's circular drive, Mr. Bishop put the car in park and stepped out. He handed his keys to a valet dressed in a red blazer and black pants. The rest of us stepped out of the car, too, and followed Mr. Bishop into the hotel restaurant. He told the skinny hostess his name and that we had dinner reservations and she escorted us to our table in the center of the room. I remembered to pull Lexi's chair out and make sure that she was comfortable before taking my seat. Mr. Bishop did the same for Kat. He watched me with judging eyes as I placed Lexi's cloth napkin into her lap.

My father had taught me well—about how a gentleman behaves in situations like this one. We'd gone out on many occasions to fancy restaurants, and I'd practiced opening doors, pulling out chairs and placing napkins into my mother's lap. I was tested and graded and when I failed, Dad would make me repeat the process over and over again until I got it right. I always dismissed the process as being a waste of time and couldn't see how it would ever benefit me. But as I glanced over my menu, I was suddenly grateful to my father for insisting that I learn how to be a gentleman.

"Looks as if your father taught you some things, Vance. You're no stranger to places like this." He smiled for the first time and it rearranged his entire face.

"Yes, sir," I said and then turned my attention to Lexi. "Would you like for me to order for you?"

She giggled as if I'd told a funny joke. "No, thank you. I always get the same thing…chicken fingers."

"Vance, you're so sweet. Isn't he just the sweetest, honey?" Kat asked her husband. "Reminds me of you when you were his age. Just the perfect little gentleman. Vance, I met Mr. Bishop when we were in college. Much like you and Lexi, we were young and in love."

"We were broke," Mr. Bishop interjected as he closed his menu. He'd obviously decided on a meal.

"We didn't care about being broke, Donnie. We just cared about being together," Kat said.

"Do you know what you're ordering, sweetheart?" He changed the subject.

"Yes, I'm gonna have the seafood pasta." Kat took one last glance at her menu and then closed it.

When the server came to take our orders, Mr. Bishop ordered a sirloin steak for himself and the seafood pasta for Kat. When he was done, he looked at me and gave me a nod. I ordered a well-done cheeseburger and the chicken fingers and fries for Lexi. Mr. Bishop asked for a bottle of chardonnay and when the server brought it over, he tasted it to make sure it was right. After he let the server know that the wine was good, she filled his glass and Kat's.

"You don't drink, do you, Vance?" he asked.

"No, sir." Not usually, I thought. Was I supposed to count the beer I had at the frat party on Friday night or the occasional cocktails I snuck during summer cookouts in our backyard? He didn't ask if I'd ever had a drink; he asked if I drank. And the answer was no.

"That's good. Alcohol is not good for you," he stated. "What about smoking? Do you smoke?"

"No, I don't smoke."

"What about those funny cigarettes?"

"Funny cigarettes?" I asked.

"He's talking about marijuana, Vance. Honey, please behave," Kat said.

"Daddy, please." Lexi gave him the evil eye.

"Hey, I'm just asking." Mr. Bishop held his hands up in surrender. "I have a right to know, don't I?"

"No, sir, I do not smoke marijuana. I don't smoke cigarettes or Blacks. I don't drink, except at a party one time I had a beer. I'm not a perfect guy. I have flaws but overall I'm a decent person. I care about your daughter very much...and I..."

My thoughts were interrupted by the girl who'd just

walked into the hotel with a group of people. They were engaged in loud conversations as they carried luggage across the shiny buffed floors. The girl looked like Tameka and was even pregnant.

"Friends of yours?" Mr. Bishop directed his attention toward the group who had approached the check-in desk.

"I thought I knew them," I admitted and then resumed my conversation. I grabbed Lexi's hand in mine. "Like I was saying, I really care about Lexi."

"I believe you, son," Mr. Bishop stated and I waited for the punch line, for the *but* that would follow. "My daughter's a smart girl and she makes good decisions. And if she has chosen you to spend some time with, then you have my blessing."

Was he serious? I exhaled. He'd had me uptight from the moment I slid into the backseat of his car. It wasn't as if Lexi and I were getting married, but still, I wanted his approval. I wanted him to like me—to see me for the person I was and not judge me. Not just because I was dating his daughter, but because Mr. Bishop had suddenly become someone that I looked up to. He seemed to have it all together and was a man who took care of his family. I respected that. Even though my father was a good role model, Mr. Bishop was also someone that I could pattern my life after.

He seemed to finally come around, ease up, and I was relieved. The conversation was pleasant after that. We seemed to have found a conversation that we were both passionate about—sports, and spent the entire time talking about basketball and football. When he found out that I was from Atlanta, we discussed Michael Vick and his fighting dogs. We both agreed that Vick had been the heartbeat of the Atlanta Falcons. And that football in Atlanta hadn't been the same since he left the team. I told Mr. Bishop about the full athletic scholarship that I'd received to Grambling and how my father had insisted on Duke.

"Should have listened to your father," he said. "Duke was a much better choice overall. Matter of fact, Grambling can't even compare."

"I disagree." I was confident. Mr. Bishop and I had hit it off, and I suddenly felt comfortable speaking my mind.

"You can disagree all you want, son. But when you get to be my age, you'll discover that your father knew exactly what was best for you. At your age, you think you got it all figured out. Unfortunately, you don't know jack. You'll figure out what I'm talking about one of these days, but by then you will have already made some stupid decisions that you can't change." He sounded just like my father. A conversation with Dad would've gone exactly like this.

Lexi smiled at me as she gossiped with her mother about some girls back home that she'd grown up with. Her mother brought her up to speed on what everybody was doing or not doing. The two of them giggled and totally ignored the conversation I was having with Mr. Bishop. Lexi was just glad that we were getting along. He was finally warming up to me and we both knew it. I gave her a smile back that let her know that she could relax. We were going to be just fine.

twenty-four

Tameka

AS we stepped inside the hotel's air-conditioned lobby, I was grateful that we were finally there. I was tired of being cramped up in the back of Calvin's father's SUV and couldn't wait to get out and stretch. Indigo, Jade, Tymia, Asia, Alyssa and I had scraped up enough cash for two rooms with double beds. With a couple of rollaway beds pulled into the room, we could all sleep comfortably for a few nights.

I lingered near the hotel's restaurant just to take in the smells. The McDonald's quarter pounder with cheese that I'd scarfed down somewhere between Birmingham and Tuscaloosa, Alabama, had worn off long ago and I was hungry again. I wanted something other than fast food. I wanted a hot meal—maybe a sirloin steak or something smothered in gravy. After checking into our room, I pulled Indi over to the restaurant so that we could check out the menu, see if they had something that would satisfy my cravings.

"May I help you?" The skinny, blonde hostess asked.

"Um, we just wanna see a menu...see what y'all got to eat," I said.

"There's a McDonald's less than a mile down the block."

She smiled a fake little smile. "Are you sure you don't want to eat there?"

"We don't want no McDonald's, boo. We would like to eat here," I insisted.

"Oh, well let me get you a menu." She disappeared across the room.

I turned to Indigo. "Ooh, let me go get y'all a menu. She should've just done that in the first place! Didn't nobody ask her about no McDonald's down the street. If we wanted McDonald's, we would've stopped at McDonald's before we got here."

"Calm down, Mama." Indigo pressed her hand against my stomach. "Let's get this baby fed before you snap out on the woman."

"She must got me mixed up!" I said and glanced around at all the faces inside the restaurant.

People were dressed in sports jackets, polo shirts and dresses, while I sported Vance's Carver High School basketball jersey, with his name plastered across the back, and a pair of denim maternity shorts. When the hostess returned with the menu, it took all of my strength not to snatch it from her hands. Instead I grabbed it and offered her the same fake smile she'd given us earlier.

"Here you go," she sang in her high-pitched voice.

"Thank you," I said reluctantly.

Indigo and I shared the menu, looking for something good to eat.

"Tameka, I might be wrong, but that sure looks like Vance over there at the table. You see them? It's the table of four."

My eyes veered in the direction that she pointed in. I knew the roundness of Vance's head and his smile. I knew him anywhere. "That is him!" I exclaimed. "But who are those people he's with?"

"I don't know," Indigo said.

"Did y'all say that Vance was here?" Jade asked, catching the tail end of the conversation as she approached.

"What's going on?" Alyssa asked.

Everyone was standing behind me as I decided to make my way across the room toward Vance. I couldn't determine if the look on his face was one of surprise, disappointment or fear. I waddled toward him proudly; couldn't wait to meet his friends or whomever he was having dinner with. He would introduce me as his girl and everyone at Grambling would finally know who his family was. My smile faded when he didn't smile back. He looked right through me, as if he didn't know who I was.

"Hey, baby," I cooed and shook from side to side. "Surprise!"

"Tameka, what are you doing here?" He didn't rise to greet me. No hello, no hugs and kisses. He seemed upset.

"I came down to surprise you for the weekend. Indi and everybody's here. See, they're right over there." I pointed to my friends who were watching my every move.

Vance glanced over at my friends. They all smiled and waved. He waved but he wasn't smiling.

"Vance, where's your manners?" Kat smiled. "Introduce us to your friend."

I didn't wait for him to say anything. It seemed that the cat had his tongue. So I extended my hand toward the nice lady. "I'm Tameka Brown, Vance's girlfriend…" I touched my belly, giggled "…and his baby mama."

"His baby mama! What?" The girl who was seated next to Vance stood and placed her hand on her hip. Her body language was that of a girl who wanted to fight.

"Yes, his baby mama." I rolled my neck like I had attitude all of a sudden. Was she hard of hearing? And why was she tripping? "And his girlfriend."

"You can't be his girlfriend," the girl said, "because I'm his girlfriend."

"Since when?" I asked.

"Since none-of-your-business. Vance, who is this?" she asked.

The cat still had his tongue so I pushed his shoulder. "Boy, will you please open your mouth and tell this hoochie who I am? I didn't come down here for all this…"

"Then why did you come down here, Tameka?"

"I came down here to kick it with you for the weekend. I thought you might be surprised," I explained, desperately wishing I hadn't come now.

"What do you have to say for yourself, Vance?" the older stuffy gentleman sitting across from Vance asked. "Is there any truth to what this girl is saying? Is this your child she's carrying?"

Vance cleared his throat. "Um, sir…there's a perfectly good explanation for all of this…I, um…"

The boy was acting as if he was temporarily insane or something. The question was a simple one yet he couldn't answer it. I glanced over at the girl who had been in my face moments earlier. She looked as if tears were starting to fill her eyes and the puzzle pieces were slowly coming together.

"So you already have a girlfriend and a baby on the way! And you never even bothered to tell me." Her voice cracked.

"I know. I should've told you, Lexi. I'm so sorry," Vance said.

"Who is she supposed to be, Vance?" I had to know.

"I'm his girlfriend." There was that attitude again, and her hands on her hips. "Didn't I tell you that earlier?"

"I can explain," Vance said.

"I'm listening," the girl he referred to as Lexi said at the same time as me.

"I'm not interested in hearing any more of this and neither is Lexi." The stuffy older man stood. "Lexi, sweetie, let's go."

The woman stood, too, and they both pushed their chairs in. Lexi acted as if she was paralyzed, as if her legs wouldn't move. She stood there for a moment longer and then reluctantly started moving toward the door.

"You're no different than any other guy, Vance. I thought you were but you're not."

"Lexi, I'm sorry," Vance said. He sounded so pitiful.

She didn't stop. Didn't turn around. She just kept moving as the older gentleman wrapped his arm around her shoulder. She rested her head on his shoulder and I knew then that he must've been her father. I started moving toward the door, too. It was so hard to face my friends after the fiasco. They looked as if they were stunned. All seven faces were in a state of disbelief and all fourteen eyes were on me. I turned to Vance.

"Is this why you came down here…to find a new girl? And party and have fun while I'm stuck at home, fat, pregnant…?"

"Tameka, I'm sorry," he said. "I didn't mean to hurt you."

"But you did, Vance. You hurt me really bad." I felt a roller coaster of emotions—hurt, disappointment, anger, sadness and embarrassment. I wanted Vance to feel those things, too. "I hate you, Vance Armstrong, and I wish I'd never met you."

With that, I left the restaurant. Needed to hurry because the tears were burning my eyes, threatening to flow. I didn't want the whole world to see me cry. I was glad that I had the key to our room and rushed to catch the next elevator.

"Tameka, wait!" Indigo yelled.

She hopped onto the elevator just in the nick of time and stood next to me.

"I feel so stupid," I whispered.

She didn't say another word, just grabbed my hand and as our fingers intertwined, we both watched as the elevator climbed its way up fourteen flights.

twenty-five

Marcus

"SO, are you supposed to be Hollywood?" I demanded an answer from Daria.

She looked at me as if I was speaking in a foreign language and laughed. "What are you talking about, Marcus?"

Sitting behind the desk at the library, punching keys on a computer, she barely looked up. I didn't want to confront her while she was at work but I had no choice. I wanted to know if she was the one sending Indigo anonymous e-mail messages.

"I don't think this is funny at all."

"Okay…so I'll stop laughing," she said even though she continued to giggle.

"Sending e-mails to people's girlfriends is not cool. Not even a little bit," I said. Everyone within earshot was looking my way but I didn't care. It didn't even matter that we were in the library. I needed to get to the bottom of this and Daria owed me some answers.

It had been three days since Indigo received the e-mail with photos attached. She refused to take my calls and wouldn't return any of my messages. Not only had guilt overtaken me, but I missed her like crazy. She was the sunshine that brightened my day each morning. Even though it was summertime, she made it a point to set her alarm just so she could wake me up and send me off to class the right way. She sent me cute little text messages all through the day, sometimes just to say "hi" or "I miss you." And at night she called to say good-night. And now I wasn't receiving any of those things. It was true—I had taken her for granted and I regretted it.

"Marcus, what are you talking about?" She lowered her voice to a whisper.

"Someone sent an e-mail to Indigo and…"

"And you think it was me." It was more of a statement rather than a question. She really had no idea what I was talking about.

"Who else would do something like that?"

"I don't know, but I don't appreciate being accused of things without someone getting their facts straight."

"I'm sorry. I'm just so…angry."

"Angry because somebody sent your girlfriend a crazy e-mail?"

"Yeah. And she won't talk to me now. I can't even get her to pick up the phone."

"I thought you were going to break things off with her anyway. I told you, it will be almost impossible dating someone in high school when you come here for your under-grad studies, Marcus."

"I didn't wanna do it this way. I didn't want to hurt her. I love her."

"Did you love her when your lips were all up against mine, Marcus?"

"What?"

"Nothing," she mumbled under her breath. She continued to log a stack of library books into a computer and avoided eye contact with me.

I turned to walk toward the door.

"Hey, Marcus," Daria said.

"Yeah?"

"I know who Hollywood is," she said.

"Who?" I walked back toward the desk.

"Your roommate, Chris," she said. "He tried to hit on my friend, Julia, and he calls himself Hollywood. Maybe you can start there."

I was shocked. Confused. Why would Chris send an e-mail to Indigo with photos attached? Actually, a better question was how did he get photos of Daria and me and why would he take them in the first place? If Daria was right, then I needed to confront Chris. I wanted to ask him why he was acting like a sick and twisted stalker. I was angry and I knew that I needed to calm down before I approached Chris, but I didn't know how. The closer I got to the dorm, the angrier I became.

As I walked briskly across the courtyard, Jae was headed my way, a backpack swung over his shoulder.

"Hey, Marcus." He seemed to always be in the best of moods; a wide grin on his face, he reached his fist out—expecting me to give him some dap. I had taught him the meaning of "dap" as well as the African American brotherly handshake. He wanted to practice it every chance he got. "What's up, my brother?"

"It's all good, Jae. What's up with you?"

Jae caused me to smile even though I wasn't in the mood for cheer. He had a way of making life seem less serious. Especially when his issues ran much deeper than mine.

"Chillin' chillin'," Jae said, using the slang I had taught him the first day I met him. He was definitely a quick study. "Where you headed, Marcus?"

"Looking for Chris. You seen him?"

"Not since I left for class this morning. Have you checked

the dining hall or The Yard?" The Yard was where students sometimes hung out. If you were looking for someone, it was a good chance you might find them there.

"Nah, I haven't checked either of those places."

"Is everything okay? You look funny."

"It's Chris. He did something really stupid and I need to find him...confront him."

"Everything he does or says is stupid. Which stupid thing did he do this time?"

Jae had a point. It wasn't unusual for Chris to do or say something stupid or inappropriate. It was as if he didn't care about anyone or anything; he just did what he pleased. I should've been able to dismiss this incident as one of those things but I couldn't. My privacy had been violated in so many ways.

"He took pictures of me and Daria...you know the girl from the library. I kissed her and he sent the photos to my girlfriend back home."

"He sent pictures to the pretty girl in Georgia...Indigo." Jae felt as if he knew Indi and she felt as if she knew him, too. They would've liked each other had they ever got the chance to meet.

"Yes, Indigo. She hates me now. Won't take my calls or return my text messages."

"Wow. And you think Chris took the photos and sent them to her?"

"I don't know if it was him for sure, but someone named Hollywood sent Indigo the e-mail. And somebody told me that Chris calls himself Hollywood." I started walking again. "So I need to find Chris."

"I'm coming, too," Jae said and started walking alongside of me.

We quickly scanned the dining hall in search of Chris only to find that he wasn't there. Making our way over to

The Yard in the afternoon heat, I wasn't surprised that he was not there, either. When we reached the dorm, I had calmed down tremendously and I was glad. But I was still anxious to find Chris. Chris sat in a chair in the corner of the room, laughing heartily as he watched a comedy rerun.

"These guys are hilarious." He held on to his stomach as he continued to laugh.

It took a lot of restraint not to grab the collar of Chris's shirt and throw him against the wall. Instead I remembered Jae's pep talk that he'd given me while walking from The Yard.

"Violence never helps, Marcus. It only makes things worse. If you're calm, you get better answers."

"But if you're choking somebody, they're more likely to give you what you want."

"And if you're choking somebody, you put your life and the lives of others in danger. Not to mention, you risk your future here at Harvard."

Okay, so he had a point. And I listened. When I saw Chris, I resisted the urge to get in his face. Instead I was calm when I sat on the edge of the sofa across from him. I stared at him with the most fearful stare that I could.

"What's your problem, dude?" he asked, taking a moment away from the TV.

"You're my problem…" I began until Jae cleared his throat to remind me of our pep talk. "Did you send photos of me and Daria to my girlfriend in Georgia?"

"What are you talking about?" Chris asked as Paul walked into the living area from his room. "What's this guy talking about, man?"

"I'm talking about someone sending inappropriate photos of me and another girl to my girlfriend. Who would be so lowdown?"

"Wasn't me, dude. I got better things to do with my time."

"Aren't you Hollywood? Isn't that your screen name?"

"I am Hollywood...on e-mail, MySpace and Facebook. But I didn't do it."

"Isn't it ironic that she received the pictures from someone who calls himself Hollywood and there's a guy who also calls himself Hollywood living in my dorm?"

"That is pretty ironic, man." Chris laughed. "And it sounds like something I would do...just for kicks...but it wasn't me."

Part of me believed him. I got the feeling that he would brag about doing something like that rather than deny it. It would make his day if someone was miserable as a result of his little sick, twisted mind and he would take pleasure in knowing that he hurt someone. But the fact that he wasn't gloating caused me to believe that he wasn't the culprit.

"Then who has access to your computer?"

"No one has access to my computer but me. My computer is locked when I'm not using it."

"I'm sorry about that entire situation, Marcus. I heard what happened," Paul said. "However, you have to decide what you want. Either you're going be with the girl here or you're going to be with your girl back home. It's dangerous to play games with either of their hearts."

"Well, I think that decision has already been made for me. My girl back home won't even talk to me, thanks to Hollywood."

"Aww, she'll come around," Chris said. "She's just pissed off right now. Give her time. You're a good dude and she'll be crazy not to talk to you."

It was actually the nicest thing Chris had ever said to me and I had to look at him just to see if there was a punch line coming...that laugh or silly grin that belonged only to him. All eyes were on him, waiting for him to say, "I'm just kidding." But he never did. He just continued to laugh at the TV.

"Chris, what's your story, man? Why are you so..." I took a moment, tried to think of the right word to describe him. There were so many choice words out there that I could've used to describe him, but only one came to mind. "Why are you so anal?"

Chris burst into laughter while the rest of us simply watched. We didn't get the joke.

"You'd be anal, too, if you had to grow up in an environment like I did. With a father who pounded your mom's head into the wall on a daily basis, and while she's screaming for him to stop, he pounds even harder. And if that's not enough, he sexually abuses..." He swallowed hard, turned the television off. He became angry; he started pacing the floor like he wanted to punch something—the wall or one of us. He started shadowboxing. "And he sexually abuses his kids."

"Your father sexually abused you?" Paul asked.

His silence was answer enough for us. He spoke volumes without even saying a word. Instead he dropped his head, and I felt sorry for him.

"It's okay, Chris," I said. "Everybody has their family issues. But you're here now...at Harvard...away from him. And after you get your degree, you don't ever have to go back there again...not if you don't want to."

"It's not that simple, Marcus. My mom is still there. And so are my two sisters. Gina is fourteen and Marlene is sixteen."

"Can't you have him arrested?" Paul asked.

"My father is very prominent and well respected in our community. He would be out of jail in less than twenty-four hours and would hire the very best attorney team in the country," Chris said. "No one would go up against him."

"If you, your mother and your sisters testified against him, he wouldn't stand a chance in court. No judge would allow him to walk," I said.

"My father *is* the judge."

"Your father's a judge and does these things to his family?" I asked.

Chris simply shook his head yes. I sighed and placed my hand over my head. Suddenly my problems didn't seem so big, not compared to Chris's problems. His were much more serious than mine and I wanted desperately to help him. But I didn't have any solutions.

"My father wanted me home for the summer. Wanted me to work as an intern for his friend's law firm. When I told him that I was going to summer school instead, he threatened to stop paying my tuition. I'm not sure if he paid it, but I'm assuming that he did because they haven't kicked me out yet."

"Have you applied for scholarships?" asked Jae.

"Most scholarships require essays, and I'm not the best writer. I can get by for a class but not competing against people who are undoubtedly much better writers than me."

"We can help you," Paul said. "Writing is my asset. I could write you an essay in my sleep."

"And I can find you some scholarships. There's lots of college money out there," I explained. "I've already received two for next fall when I attend Harvard full-time. My father won't have to come out of pocket for anything during my first two years."

"Why would you do that for me?" Chris asked. "Why would you help me when I've been rude and obnoxious toward you, got you put out of a cab one night?"

"Yeah, you did do all of those things, didn't you?" I laughed.

"It's not your fault that you're so…so anal," Paul suggested.

"Yeah, I would probably be anal, too, if I had a father like yours. My father is so different. He's not rich or prominent, although he is respected. He has a property management business that he struggles with. He runs around town making repairs to these beat-up old houses and he allows his tenants to pay rent at their leisure." I laughed. "But they love him and he always manages to make ends meet. I wouldn't trade my old man for any other dad in the world."

"You're lucky," Chris mumbled. "Some of us aren't as fortunate. I hate my father. Sometimes I wish he was dead."

"That's deep, man," I said.

There was a short uncomfortable silence. Paul and I were at a loss of words for Chris. There was nothing more that we could say that would change what he'd gone through with this father.

Paul changed the subject. "Now if you could just get your girlfriend back, your life would be perfect, right, Marcus?"

"I didn't realize how much she meant to me until she was gone," I explained. "I thought that I needed someone who was more mature. Someone who wasn't in high school but who I could have intellectual conversations with...and who understood me. But the truth is Indigo does understand me. She knows what I'm going to say before I even say it. She knows what I'm thinking and what I'm feeling."

"I wonder who sent that e-mail," Paul said.

"I don't know, but if it came from my e-mail address, then it should still be in my sent box, right?" Chris stood, went into his room and came back with his laptop computer. "Let's see if there's an outgoing message."

He sat down, started clicking buttons on his computer until he was logged into his e-mail account. After a few moments of pecking, he looked up at me.

"There's an outgoing message here."

"Let me see." I stood over Chris's shoulder. Paul came over and looked, too.

I read the words that were in the outgoing e-mail message in all lowercase:

indigo, i guess your golden boy ain't so golden after all...check out these photos. with deepest sympathy, hollywood

"Open the pictures. I want to see them," I told Chris.

Chris double-clicked on the photos that were attached to the outgoing e-mail. The first was an intimate shot of Daria and me in Harvard Yard. My arm was wrapped around her shoulder as she gazed into my eyes, her fingertip wiping something from my face. I remembered the exact moment— I wanted to kiss her but the sound of a passing airplane interrupted the moment and we started talking about something else. The second was a photo of Daria and me in the park. She was pressed against the tree and my body and my lips were pressed against hers.

I could have argued that the photos were taken before Indigo became my girl. That they were photos that were taken before I moved to College Park; before I even knew who Indigo Summer was. But the truth of the matter was I was wearing the jersey she'd bought me for my last birthday. And in the third photo, as Daria wrapped her skinny arms around my waist, I twirled the charm that hung from a chain around my neck—the silver charm that was a half heart inscribed with the words I love you. Indigo wore the other half of the heart around her neck on a silver chain. I'd given it to her before I left; a symbol that she had the other half of my heart and I had hers. And when we were back together, in the same state, the heart would be whole again. She had undoubtedly recognized that charm immediately.

I touched my half of the heart that dangled around my neck and wondered if the heart would be whole again after this. "Who do you think sent this?" I asked Chris.

"I don't know. But it pisses me off that someone was able to tap into my computer like that. I feel violated."

"Hello, good people," Derrick said as he came through the door. He dropped his backpack at the door. "What's going on?"

He became an immediate suspect in my eyes. Derrick was a computer whiz. He told us that the first day we met. "I could tap into Fort Knox if I wanted to." Those were his words. Not to mention he wanted Daria from the moment he first laid eyes on her. His ego was shattered when she didn't want him, too. It was no secret he was jealous of me. After all, I had two beautiful girls and he couldn't even pull one.

"Why did you do it?" I asked Derrick. Everyone in the room gave me strange looks, thought I'd lost my mind.

"Do what?" Derrick asked. I could see right through his act of innocence.

"Marcus, what are you saying?" Paul asked. "Are you suggesting that Derrick sent the e-mail?"

"I know he did," I explained. "It all adds up now. It had to be someone who lives in this dorm. Someone who had access to Chris's computer."

"But I lock my computer when I'm not using it, Marcus. I never forget," Chris said.

"But if you're a computer whiz, you can tap into anyone's computer...even when it's locked," I explained.

"And he wanted Daria for himself," Jae added.

"But she wouldn't give him the time of day." I felt like the older white-haired lady on *Murder, She Wrote* as I began to crack the case.

Derrick was silent. With his hands stuffed into the pocket of his khaki shorts, he just stood there with a smug look on his face. He didn't deny the accusations.

"Could you really do something like this?" Paul asked Derrick.

"It wasn't fair...the way he was running around here with a beautiful girl chasing after him...all the while keeping another beautiful girl at bay while he had his fun. He's not this wonderful person that everybody thinks he is, and I thought someone should know."

"So you send an anonymous e-mail to his girlfriend? That's undoubtedly a violation of the men's code. That was a punk move!" Paul said, and I was surprised at his choice of words. *Punk move* didn't seem like words that would ever be in his vocabulary. I was proud of him, though.

"A punk move?" I smiled at Paul.

"Yes, Marcus, a punk move," Paul said, but he wasn't smiling.

"What's a punk move, Marcus?" Jae asked.

"Not now, Jae. I'll explain later."

"You tapped into my computer without my knowledge? You little…" Chris leapt from his chair, tackled Derrick to the floor.

Before anyone could say another word, Chris had punched Derrick in the face. The two of them tussled on the floor for a few minutes. Chris released the bottled-up anger and gave Derrick the beating that he should've saved for his abusive father. We all stood there for a few minutes, allowing Chris the opportunity to get licks for all of us. Finally, Paul grabbed Chris while I held Derrick down on the floor with the sole of my shoe. I wanted to stomp him—to release some of my own bottled-up anger but decided against it. Violence never solved anything.

When the Harvard Police burst through the door, it was my foot against Derrick's chest that caused them to aggressively pull my arms behind my back and slap handcuffs on to my wrists.

"What are you doing, man? I haven't done anything!" I tried to plead my case.

"Officer, I can affirm he didn't do anything," Paul said.

"Actually, it was me who assaulted him," Chris said. "If you want to arrest someone, arrest me."

We all knew that if Chris was arrested, he would be put out of the summer program and not be able to return to Harvard next fall.

"It's really quite funny, sir...you're going to be largely amused when you hear this," Paul said. "They were playing around, horseplay if you will. You know how carried away boys can get. I've told them time and again to stop all of the roughhousing...that someone might get hurt, but they don't listen. Wrestling is a sport for a coliseum or a field house I told them..."

"Were you assaulted by either of these men, sir?" the officer asked Derrick.

"Um..." Derrick hesitated...looked around the room at each of our faces one by one; he knew he'd better give the right response or he'd pay. "We were horsing around and it got a little carried away. I was not assaulted by either of these men."

"So you're not interested in pressing charges?" the officer asked.

"No. No, of course not. Like I said, it was all in fun." He gave the officer a fake laugh.

"We were close by when one of your neighbors called and said it sounded like someone was fighting," one officer said as the other one released my handcuffs. If we have to come back out here because you can't control your *horseplay*, then somebody's going to jail."

"Won't happen again, Officer. You have my word." Paul escorted them to the door.

In an instant, they were gone and I exhaled. The situation could've been worse. Chris and I could've spent the night in jail and completely screwed up our futures at Harvard. All Derrick had to do was admit to being assaulted and his testimony would've changed our lives forever. But he had protected us instead. He must've felt some level of guilt for causing the disturbance in the first place.

"I'm sorry about the computer, man," Derrick said to Chris. "And, Marcus, I'm sorry about sending the photos to your girlfriend. I was angry. And jealous. I wanted Daria to like me the way she liked you. It messed with my head because I was used to girls chasing after me. When she didn't, I couldn't take it."

Was he serious? Girls couldn't possibly be chasing after him. He didn't even keep his fro tight, and girls were sticklers for personal hygiene. You had to come correct when you approached them—no funky breath, no corny clothes or shoes and definitely no nappy hair.

"How did you find Indigo's e-mail?"

"She has a MySpace page and a Facebook account," he said matter-of-factly. Grinning, he added, "She's got some hot pictures on MySpace, by the way. Have you seen them?"

"Hey, watch yourself, bro," I warned.

"She's way more beautiful than Daria any day of the week. What were you thinking anyway?" Derrick asked.

"I just got caught up, man. Could happen to anybody."

"Now he's got to figure out how to get her back," Paul said.

Paul was right. I needed a plan of action. Poor judgment had caused the girl of my dreams to slip right through my fingers. I knew that I needed to start praying because it was going to take an act of God to get her back.

twenty-six

Vance

The taxi from the hotel in Ruston back to campus cost me twenty-three bucks and some change. Killed my spending cash but it was better than walking. In one evening, my life had been turned upside down and I didn't know what to expect next. As I sat there on the edge of my bed, my phone in hand, I thought about calling my mother. She always knew what to do in the toughest situations. And she was the only person in the whole world who wasn't so quick to judge me and would have some good advice for me. She would tell me how to move forward, because at the moment I was stuck.

"Hey, Ma, it's me…Vance," I said when she picked up her phone.

"Hello, baby. How are you?" I could hear the smile in her voice. I always made her happy when I called home, which was rare. She usually ended up calling me just to make sure I was all right and didn't need for anything.

"I'm okay. Just got a lot on my head right now. Feeling a little down."

"Talk to me. What's going on?"

"I messed up everything, Ma. I came down here and lost

my focus. I started dating this girl, Lexi. And I really, really like her, Ma, but I kept feeling guilty about liking her so much because of Tameka."

"Baby, there's nothing wrong with meeting another girl that you like—"

I interrupted her because I wanted to get it all out, didn't want to forget one detail. "I mean, I respect Tameka and I want to handle my responsibility…you know, as a man and take care of my kid…"

"Did you tell Tameka how you feel…that you met someone else?"

"No, I didn't."

"Did you tell this other girl…what's her name?"

"Lexi."

"Did you tell Lexi about Tameka and that you were about to become a father?"

"No, ma'am. I just kept juggling both of them and hoping that I never had to tell either of them anything. But tonight, it all exploded in my face."

"What happened?"

"Tameka showed up here, in Grambling. I had no idea that she was coming. She popped up at the restaurant where I was having dinner with Lexi and her parents—"

"So you've met this girl's parents?"

"Yes. I went to her hometown for the Fourth of July weekend and made a complete fool of myself. But that's another story," I told her. "But tonight, I was having dinner with them again, and I really think her father was starting to like me—"

"You must really like this girl if you're trying to impress her father."

"I do really like her, Ma, but can I finish the story?"

She was driving me crazy with the interruptions. I had so much to tell her and I needed to get it all out.

"Of course, I won't interrupt again."

"Anyway, I'm having dinner with Lexi and her parents, and Tameka pops up out of nowhere, waddles over to the table and practically let the whole world know that I was her baby daddy—"

"Well, you are her baby daddy, sweetie." She chuckled.

"Ma, I was trying so hard to impress Lexi's father. And he was finally warming up to me, even after the fiasco in Jackson, Mississippi. He had already been skeptical about me...thinking that I wasn't good enough for his daughter or something—"

"Well, you can lose that thought. You are good enough! You're a spectacular young man with a bright future. Your father and I are proud of your accomplishments. You've made good grades in school, received a full scholarship to a four-year college—"

"And got a girl pregnant..."

"Okay, you made a mistake, sweetheart. We all make mistakes. I have news for you. You're going to continue to make mistakes as long as you live. But you have to correct your mistakes and move on. That's why, for your first year in college, your father and I will handle your financial responsibilities as far as the baby's concerned, just like we said. When the baby's born, you will be an active part of his or her life. I'm talking about spending quality time and bonding with the child as much as possible. Next school year, you will get a part-time job so that you can handle your responsibilities on your own. It's not the end of the world, Vance."

"Feels like it."

"Let me tell you where you went wrong, honey. And then maybe you can focus again," Mom said. "It wasn't fair to Tameka to keep her hanging on...hoping and wishing that you, her and the baby were going to be this big happy family once the baby was born—"

"I couldn't—"

"Let me finish," she interrupted. "You knew long before you went away to school that you weren't in love with that girl. I knew it because I know you. There was no spark in your eyes or excitement in your voice when you spoke about her. Not like this new girl. Yet, you tried so hard to be noble...to do the right thing and that just means that you have character. All that's wonderful, but, baby, in essence you strung her along...."

"I didn't want to hurt her feelings."

"Sometimes we hurt people more when we're not honest with them. And you weren't very honest with Tameka and as a result you ended up hurting her more. You created a mess. And now you have this new girl, Lexi, who is walking around campus thinking that she's the only girl in your life. But the truth is, you've got this huge secret that you don't even bother to share with her. You didn't give her a say in the matter. You took away her choices. What if she wasn't interested in dating a guy who had a baby on the way?"

"That's what I was afraid of...that she wouldn't want me. That's why I didn't tell her."

"It wasn't up to you to make that decision for her. She deserved an opportunity to make her own choices and you took that away."

"I didn't want to lose her."

"It wasn't just about you, sweetie, and that's how you made it. Nobody had any choices but you. You made choices for both of them and that simply wasn't fair."

"So how do I fix it, Ma? They both hate me right now. They won't answer my calls or my text messages."

"What is it that you want, honey? You tell me."

"I want to do the right thing and be a father to my child when he or she gets here. I want to continue to be friends with Tameka. I want her to forgive me. But I don't think a relationship is the best thing for us right now."

"Okay."

"And I want Lexi to be my girl. Ma, I really like her. She's smart, she's athletic and she's funny. I can be myself around her. I can say what I wanna say and she doesn't get all weird-acting like other girls. And did I mention that she's pretty?"

"You didn't mention it but I figured that was one of her attributes." Mom laughed.

"I can't think of any girl that I have ever liked better."

"Okay. Your problems really aren't that huge, Vance. Here's what you have to do. Is Tameka still there?"

"I think so."

"You've got to get some one-on-one time with her. You do everything you can to get with her before she leaves. You apologize profusely for being inconsiderate and dishonest. And then you let her know what your plans are...that you fully intend to take care for your child but a relationship with her is not what you would like right now. She's going to be hurt but years from now she'll respect you for it."

"That's not gonna be easy."

"Of course not. Some things in life just aren't easy, but what matters is that you do the right thing."

"What about Lexi?"

"If Lexi is this wonderful person that you say she is...she'll be all right. She'll come around. If it's meant to be, it will be. You apologize to her for being dishonest. You tell her how you feel about her and let nature take its course."

"What if she doesn't take me back? What if she doesn't accept my apology?"

"Sweetie, you're still young. You're handsome. There are a million other Lexis out there just waiting to get a shot at Vance Armstrong."

"But I don't want a million other Lexis…I want this one."

"Well, you have to let her know that," Mom said. "I hope you feel better, son."

"I do, Ma. Thank you. You're always there for me, no matter what. Even when I mess up."

"That's my job."

"I feel much better, but I got a lot of work to do."

"You can handle it, Counselor. I believe in you." I loved Mom's new nickname for me—*Counselor*. It sounded good, especially since some judge would be calling me that someday. It reminded me of why I came to Grambling in the first place—to get my undergrad studies over with so that I could go to law school and follow in my mother's footsteps.

I had my focus back. I knew what I had to do and I couldn't wait to get it done. The sooner I got to it, the sooner I could get on with my life. After hanging up with Mom, I gave Tameka's cell phone one last call. I would leave her a message and let her know that I wanted to meet her somewhere and talk, if she was interested in hearing what I had to say. For the tenth time, I received her voice mail and decided to leave her one last message.

"Tameka, it's Vance. Of course you already know that. I'm sure you're sitting there looking at the screen and pressing the 'ignore' button every time you see my name. Um…I really need to talk to you…about our future and the future of our baby. I know it's late, but I was wondering if you could meet me in front of the football field at ten o'clock. That's thirty minutes from now. Anyway, I hope you show up."

I hung up. Hoped that Tameka would get my message in time.

twenty-seven

Tameka

sean was the perfect gentleman when he drove me to Burger King for a bite to eat. After seeing Vance and his little girlfriend at the hotel's restaurant having dinner like it was nothing, I no longer wanted to eat at that restaurant. As a matter of fact, I lost my appetite altogether. Wanted to simply sleep the rest of the day away. I regretted coming to Grambling at all. I couldn't believe I'd let my friends talk me into the trip. It was so much better not knowing the truth. At least when I was in Atlanta I was happy. Coming here changed everything for the worse.

"You gotta answer his call at some point," Sean said as he watched me stare at the screen of my cell phone. Vance had called at least ten times, and each time I let it roll into voice mail. Unlike the other nine times, this time he left a message.

"I was so embarrassed today. I went strutting into that restaurant and left there feeling like a fool."

"No, I remember him looking like the fool. He had two cute girls standing there, and he didn't leave there with either one them."

"You thought she was cute?" I asked, remembering the caramel-colored girl who had called herself Vance's girlfriend.

"She was aiight." Sean grinned. "Not cute as you, though."

We sat in Calvin's daddy's SUV with Grambling University's Tiger Radio 91.5 playing softly on the stereo. Gerald Levert sang a sweet ballad as we sat in Burger King's parking lot, eating burgers and French fries.

"It's okay if you think she's cute. Vance obviously does, too." I forced a smile. Talking to Sean was easy. He was sweet. "Thanks for dinner, by the way."

"I wouldn't really call Burger King dinner. Especially for a pregnant woman who needs plenty of vegetables and fruits. You won't find any of those things in a Whopper. And the grease is gonna clog the baby's arteries."

"You sound like my mother."

"Well, somebody has to take Mel's place since she's not here. Somebody's gotta take care of you."

I wanted to call Mommy so bad when everything went down with Vance. After all, she was my best friend. But I couldn't let her know where I was. Not that she would kill me or anything. But I didn't want to put her in a bad position with my friends' parents. She would have to tell their parents where we were and I couldn't have that. She would be mad at first but she would understand.

"I wanted to call her today but I didn't want my friends to get into trouble."

"Yeah, that wouldn't be good. Your friends would be grounded for the rest of the summer, and my boy Cal wouldn't be able to hook up with your friend Jade. He really likes her, you know."

"Yeah? Well I think she likes him, too."

"And I like you, Tameka. I know a lot of crazy stuff happened today and you got a lot on your head, but I want you to know that I'm here for you. And when everything calms down, I'll still be here for you."

"Thank you."

I kept pretending that I wasn't anxious to check the voice mail message that Vance had left. I kept trying to use restraint and tell myself that I didn't care about what he had to say. But deep down inside, I wanted to hear his voice. Wanted to know if he was sorry, if he regretted his actions. Wanted to know where we stood and where we were going from here. I called my voice mail service. Listened to his message.

"He wants me to meet him on campus at the football field...at ten o'clock," I told Sean.

We both glanced at the digital clock on the dash of the SUV. It was nine-thirty.

"You wanna meet him? I'll drive you over there," said Sean.

"I wanna hear what he has to say." I shrugged. "I don't know...call me crazy."

"That's cool. Let's go."

As I walked across the football field, Vance sat in the middle of the bleachers wearing a tank top, basketball shorts and a cap on his head backward. He watched as I made my way toward him. When I reached him, he stood and helped me climb the few steps up into the bleachers. I sat down beside him and he grabbed my hand.

"I'm sorry, Tameka. I didn't mean to hurt you," he said and my heart instantly started to melt.

"I'm fine now," I said.

"I wasn't trying to hurt you," he said.

"What's up with that girl saying she was your girlfriend?"

He became quiet and looked away. When he turned back around, his eyes were watery. "Because she is my girl. At least she was before tonight."

His words cut through my heart like a sharp knife. Any hopes and dreams I had of a future with Vance were being destroyed at that moment.

I pulled my hand away. "You asked her to be your girl when you already had a girl?"

"Tameka, I really care about you...and the baby..." Vance pulled a pair of sunglasses out the pocket of his shorts; placed them on his face. "But I don't think that a relationship between us would be good right now. I mean, I want to be there for you when you have the baby and all. I want to have a relationship with my child...if you'll let me...and everything...but..."

"But you don't want *me,* right?" I asked. The tears that had built up in the corners of my eyes were threatening to fall. I tried with all my might to hold them back but they fell down my cheeks anyway.

"I think we should just be friends," he said. "Tameka, I think that you are so brave, just carrying a baby for all this time is a big deal. And I'm grateful to you for it. Grateful that you didn't abort him *or* her...."

"Her!" I said as the tears began to flow harder. They didn't care that I was trying to be tough. "It's a girl, Vance. Yes, I knew the sex of the baby for a long time and didn't tell you. I wanted to surprise you but what difference does it really make now, right? I've been doing that a lot lately...trying to surprise you...and every time I do, I'm the one who ends up with the surprise."

"So it's a girl?" he asked, and then had the nerve to touch my stomach. Part of me wanted to remove his hand from touching me, but I didn't. "Tameka, I didn't handle things the right way. When I came down here it was just so much going on...parties every weekend. Girls everywhere. I didn't know how to be faithful to you."

"You have to want to be faithful, Vance. And you obviously didn't want to!"

"I got a lot of growing up to do."

I searched my purse for a tissue. Found two. Handed one to Vance and wiped tears from my own eyes with the other one.

"We both have a lot of growing up to do," I admitted.

"My parents are going to make sure that you and the baby are taken care of financially during my first year of school. When I get in my sophomore year, I'm going to get a job and try to handle my own responsibilities."

"Yeah, whatever, Vance," I mumbled. Financial support for me and the baby just didn't seem all that important at the moment. It was more important that my world was falling apart and I didn't know how to stop it.

Changing the subject, Vance said, "Who's that dude over there…that brought you here?"

"His name is Sean. He's a friend of mine." I glanced over at Sean as he sat in the SUV with the door open listening to the stereo and talking on his cell phone. "I asked him to bring me, just in case anything jumped off." I laughed through tears.

"Yeah, right. I won't hurt you again, Tameka." Vance pulled me into his arms, held me tightly. It felt like old times, if just for a moment.

"I gotta go, Vance."

He tried to help me down from the bleachers but I pulled away. I didn't need his help. I was on my own now, so I wanted him to let me be. As I walked away he stood there, a pair of shades covering his face. I could feel him watching me and I wondered what he was thinking, feeling. Wondered if he realized that he was making a big mistake by letting me go.

"Hey, Tameka," he called.

"Yeah?" I turned to find those big brown eyes staring right at me, his shades now in his hand.

"Can I come into the delivery room when you have our baby?"

"I don't know, Vance. I'll have to think about it."

I didn't know much about anything at that moment, except that my world was slowly crumbling before my eyes and I didn't know what on earth to do about it.

twenty-eight

Marcus

I **finished** my last load of laundry just before retiring to my bedroom. Jae was still up, his night-light shining bright on his nightstand, his nose stuck deep into his Calculus book. We had all been a little cranky over the past few days as we studied profusely for our final exams. High school students that had attended Harvard for the summer would soon be going home, back to life as we knew it—in less than a week.

I was going to miss my roommates, especially Jae, my Korean friend who was now a master in Ebonics. He knew how to do the handshake that is only shared amongst brothers—*African American brothers*. His favorite phrase was "chillin' chillin'," and before long he was saying crazy stuff, like asking Chris, "What up, fool?"

Jae had become a good friend, helping me with my studies and talking me through some difficult times. We stayed up half the night talking about my problems with Indigo one night, and I couldn't count the number of times he'd vented about the girl he loved in Korea. He'd accepted the fact that he would never spend his life with her—she was promised to someone else—but he would never forget her. I told him that there were other girls just waiting for him to come back to Harvard. There weren't that many to choose from during a short summer's stay, but I would be willing to bet that pickings wouldn't be so thin when he came back next fall. He just chuckled as if I'd told a joke.

I hoped that we would be roommates again but there were no guarantees. It was true that Harvard liked to mix things up a bit. They were big on having students get to know people from different cultures, which is why they often paired English-speaking students up with students who did not speak English. The next time around I'd probably end up bunking with a bunch of people from Hong Kong or Bangladesh.

In a short time, I'd managed to find Chris a laundry list of scholarship opportunities and he'd applied for several of them. Staying up well past midnight every night for a week straight, we all sat around in our common room putting the finishing touches on Chris's essays. As a group, we'd all made the trip to the post office with him, just to make sure the applications were stamped with first-class postage before they were shipped off to where they belonged. It was a good chance that Chris would finally break free from his controlling and sick father, who continuously made his life a living hell. I felt sorry for his family. They were in prison and didn't even know it. Hopefully his sisters would eventually grow up and leave for college. That way they might even escape from him. But unfortunately, that would leave his mother to fight for her own life, and that was sad.

I would miss Paul when I went home to Atlanta. On an average day in the hood, I would never have met anyone like Paul Chapman, with his strong British accent. He was the levelheaded one of all of us and kept us grounded. He was the voice of reason when the rest of our teenage brains had lost their reasoning power. Paul was not much of a talker, but when he did talk you knew that it was important. Like the night after my altercation with Derrick. Paul was the one who reminded me that the love between me and Indigo should be able to withstand tough things. Otherwise it might not be true love. I hoped he was right. Paul was a roommate that I wouldn't mind sharing my space with again, but the chances of that were slim to none. With my luck, I'd probably get stuck with a roommate like Derrick. He was definitely someone I wasn't interested in rooming with ever again.

I opened my chemistry book, pulled out my handwritten notes that I'd jotted down during my professor's lecture and studied for my upcoming exam. When I got bored, I tossed an M&M at Jae and then pretended I didn't know where it came from. He looked over at me, threw it back.

"Marcus, you have to grow up," he said.

"What are you talking about, man? I didn't do anything."

"I'm going to miss you, Marcus."

"I will probably miss you, too." I laughed. "I'll miss your loud snores...."

"I don't snore," he protested. "Do I?"

"Some nights I can barely sleep for your snores. Couple of times I was late for school, had bags underneath my eyes from being awake all night. I hope your next roommate snores loud, too, so that he can drown you out!"

"I hope my next roommate is Marcus Carter," Jae said.

"Not a chance. The chances of that happening would be the same as Indigo forgiving me and taking me back."

"She will take you back. You have to believe that."

"Thanks, Jae, but I'm not so sure. You didn't hear her voice on the other end of that phone. She was pretty mad...and hurt...."

"She will change her mind."

"I hope you're right. If she doesn't I'm coming to Korea and hunt you down."

"Marcus, will you e-mail me during the school year? I really would like for us to stay in touch."

"Of course, Jae. Mos def, we'll keep in touch."

"Mos def?" he asked, not understanding my choice of words.

"Yeah, short for most definitely."

"You have taught me so much. I really appreciate it."

"Don't mention it, bro. That's what I'm here for." I laughed and then stuck my nose into my book and studied.

When my phone buzzed, I looked at the screen. Daria. I glanced over at Jae before picking up.

"Talk to me," I said.

"Hey, Marcus. What's going on?"

"Studying. What about you?"

"I was about to head over to the coffee shop. Wondered if you wanted to hang out?"

I thought about it for a moment. The coffee shop is where all of my problems started. Hanging out with Daria wasn't really in my best interest. I wanted my girl back and the only way of making that happen was to get rid of the things that caused me problems. I was attracted to Daria; there was no denying that. She was beautiful and smart—who wouldn't be interested in her? But after losing Indi, I knew that Daria wasn't the girl for me.

"I really need to study."

"We won't hang out for long. I just want a chai green tea really bad, and I don't wanna ride the 'T' by myself. Will you go with me?"

I checked my watch. It was seven-thirty. The night was still young. I glanced over at Jae who looked up at me with judging eyes. I wanted to stand strong and do the right thing, but I didn't have any willpower. "I'll meet you downstairs," I finally mumbled; I didn't want Jae to hear me.

"Okay, Marcus, I'll see you in a minute," Daria said and then she was gone.

As I slowly shut my book, Jae's eyes were on me. "Don't say a word. I already know," I told him.

"You're playing with fire, Marcus. You must call her back right now and decline the invitation."

"Can't do that, man." I stood, slipped a pair of flip-flops on to my feet. "I'll be back shortly."

Daria looked breathtaking in her flirty pink dress that just barely touched her knees. Her legs were shiny with baby oil and her hair was in a curly ponytail. Wearing a pair of loose basketball shorts, an old T-shirt and flip-flops, I looked underdressed in comparison to her.

"Wow, you look good," I told her. "Got me looking like a bum. If I'd known I was supposed to dress up, I would have."

"You look fine, Marcus. It doesn't really matter what you wear, you are very handsome all the time." She smiled a beautiful smile. "I've missed you. You avoiding me?"

"Somewhat." I laughed, but I thought I should be honest with Daria. Let her know what I was really thinking. "It's dangerous hanging out with you, girl. That's why I gotta stop. This is going to be my last time seeing you. I'm going home soon, and I have to patch things up with my girlfriend."

"You mean she's still mad about the photos?"

"Yeah, the photos."

"I'm really sorry about that whole thing, Marcus. I guess Chris turned out to be a real snake in the grass. I knew that he had problems, especially after that incident of getting us put out of a cab," she said as we walked across the courtyard. "What sick, twisted person would hide behind trees just to get a shot of us kissing and then send them to your girlfriend?"

She threw me off with her question. I'd never mentioned to Daria that someone had sent pictures of us kissing to Indigo. In fact, I'd never mentioned photos at all. I'd simply told her that someone had sent Indigo an e-mail.

"How did you know there were photos attached?" I asked her.

"Because you told me. Remember? That day you came into the library…all huffy and stuff, and said that someone had taken photos of us kissing and sent them to your girl-friend. You were so mad, and very rude to me, by the way. But I forgive you, Marcus."

"I never mentioned that there were photos attached to the e-mail, Daria. How did you know that?"

"Marcus, don't get all technical. You said it. If you didn't say it, then I just figured that it was obvious someone sent photos."

"It wasn't obvious," I said. Stopped dead in my tracks and looked at her. She was a liar and a sneak, and suddenly I saw her through a different set of eyes. "What…were you and Derrick working together to destroy my life?"

"Your life, Marcus? You can't be serious. We're talking about a high school crush here." She giggled. "Derrick told me that you would get a kick out of the whole thing. He said that you guys play tricks on each other all the time."

"And you thought it was a pretty good idea, too, huh?"

"I thought that if we could get rid of that little girl back in College Park, then you would finally realize that you and I made a much better couple."

"Is that what you thought?"

"It's true, Marcus. Your friend Derrick thought…"

"Don't even mention his name to me again. I don't even know Derrick like that. And he's definitely not someone that I consider a friend. And now that I'm thinking about it, shoot, neither are you," I said and started walking backward toward my dorm. "I gotta go."

"I thought we were going to get coffee."

"Maybe Derrick will go with you. He wants to hook up with you anyway. If he's in his room, I'll send him down. And the two of you can go have chai green teas together. Matter of fact…" I don't know what made me pull my wallet out of my back pocket, pull out a five-dollar bill and throw it at Daria "…drinks are on me."

I started jogging toward my building, never looked back. Didn't know if she picked up the money off the ground or not. I wanted to go back and get it; I didn't have money to throw away like that. I was already down to my last twenty. Right before I went into the building, I stole a glance back to see if she was gone and if she'd picked up my money. She was, in fact, gone and my five-dollar bill was still lying there on the ground. I rushed back, picked it up while making sure that nobody was watching, stuck it into my pocket like a thief in the night and then walked away.

twenty-nine

Vance

MY back against the wall near the gymnasium, tossing a basketball into the air, I stood in waiting. Masculine-looking girls much bigger than Lexi passed by, engaged in conversations about basketball and who knew what else. One girl with hair shorter than mine, and biceps and triceps the size of Dwight Howard's, looked my way and gave me a wink as she passed with her gym bag thrown across her shoulder. I cringed when she blew me a kiss. When I spotted Lexi, she was running her mouth with her friend Jessie and another girl from the team. She looked my way and I smiled. When she didn't return the smile, I knew she was still mad.

"Can I see you for a minute?" I asked when she passed. She ignored me and kept walking.

"You can talk to me, baby." A girl wearing a long ponytail, gym shorts and a Los Angeles Lakers jersey looked my way. "We can talk all night long."

When all of her girls started laughing, I was embarrassed. Wondered if I should continue to make a fool of myself.

"Lexi! Can I talk to you for a minute?"

"Gone ahead and talk to the man, Lexi," one of her girls said. She stopped walking, turned around and came back toward me. "What could you possibly want to talk to me about?" she asked.

"I'm sorry." That was all I could think of at the moment. The whole speech that I had rehearsed in the mirror for the past two days had escaped me.

"You said that on my voice mail fifty times already," she said.

"I know that I was wrong for not telling you about Tameka and the baby...."

"Woo...now, that's an understatement. You were so wrong that I can't even look at you." She looked up at the ceiling as she talked.

"I told Tameka that I would handle my responsibilities as far as the baby is concerned, but that we can't be in a relationship anymore. I told her that we can't be together because...I'm in love with someone else."

"Really?" she asked sarcastically. "Now who would that be, Vance? Shay or some other hoochie on this campus who's willing to drop her panties for you?"

"It's you, Lexi. I'm in love with you."

Her face softened. She finally looked at me, probably wanted to see if I was being honest or not. People's eyes didn't lie and she looked right into mine. "Well...you know what? Whatever you feel for me will pass. Now if you'll excuse me, I have to go."

She turned to walk away but I grabbed her hand. It wasn't surprising when she didn't pull it away. She still cared for me, I knew it. But her pride wouldn't let her give in. I held on to her hand as she faced the opposite direction and avoided eye contact.

"You know you still care for me," I whispered. I was close enough to her that I was sure she felt my breath on her neck. I wanted to plant kisses all up and down her spine. She didn't deny or agree with my comment. "Give me a chance to make this up to you. I can be faithful, Lexi. I can be a stand-up guy. Yes, I do have a baby on the way. And I plan on being a great father to my daughter. But don't judge me based on that. Give me a chance."

Little by little she softened. Her heart was melting for me, I just knew it. I decided not to press the issue any more. I had made my point and the ball was in her court. She was a ball player, so she knew that when the ball was in your court you didn't sleep on it—you take it and run with it. You slam-dunk it if you can.

"You think about it, Lexi. I'm not a bad dude and you know it. I just made some mistakes. I really hope that you can find it in your heart to forgive me. I can't apologize for having a baby on the way, but I apologize for not telling you the truth. I was wrong. But if you search your heart, you know deep down inside of there that you love me, that I'm the guy for you. That I did it because I didn't want to lose you. I've never felt this way about a girl before and I probably never will." I slowly released her hand, her fingertips lingered against mine. "I don't wanna pressure you, but you know where to find me if you change your mind."

I walked away. Didn't look back. I wanted to leave Lexi with some things to think about. I had said all that I could say, and even if she didn't take me back, I had attempted to make things right. And for that, I felt good.

I stepped into the empty gymnasium, dribbled the basketball in between my legs and then tossed it into the hoop. It went in with a swooshing sound. I grabbed it, bounced it around and tossed it into the hoop again. I did this until I got bored and then took a seat on the bleachers. With my elbows on my knees and my face buried in the palms of my hands, I sat there for a moment. Wondered how my life had gotten so messed up.

I stood and headed for the door. In order to let off some aggression, I pushed the door open as hard as I could and sent Lexi on a one-way trip to the floor holding her nose. She was on her way into the gym before I gave her a concussion.

"Baby, I'm sorry!" I kneeled next to her and grabbed her head into my hands. "What were you doing on the other side of the door?"

"Coming in there to see you," she mumbled.

"Are you okay?"

"You killed my nose, man. Why'd you push the door so hard?"

"I was letting off some steam because my girl won't talk to me."

"She was on her way into the gym to talk to you until you assaulted her with the door." She gave me a half smile and held onto her nose.

I grabbed her in my arms, carried her inside the gym and over to the bleachers and laid her on the bottom step. I pulled my T-shirt over my head, gathered it into a ball and placed it underneath Lexi's head.

"I'm glad you were looking for me," I whispered.

"I figured it was time to stop being so stubborn. Plus I missed you."

"Do you forgive me?"

"Yes. But I'm not playing with you, Vance. There will be no more secrets between us. You have to tell me what's going on. Even if you think it will hurt my feelings."

"Okay."

"And there will be no other girls, but me. No Shays, no Tamekas. Just Lexi Bishop."

"That's cool. I don't want nobody but you."

"Well, if you ever decide that you do...want somebody else, then all you have to do is tell me. Okay?"

"Okay, I promise," I told her.

I was just happy that we were having a conversation. It had been three days since she last spoke to me and it had been torture. But her voice was like music to my ears as she caught me up on everything that had taken place in her life over the past few days. She told me how she felt when she saw Tameka walk into the restaurant and waddle over to our table. We laughed about the looks on her parents' faces when they first laid eyes on Tameka, although it wasn't funny at the time. I told her that I wanted to crawl under the table and never surface again. I was glad that we were able to laugh about uncomfortable things like that.

After Lexi's nose felt a little better, she sat up. I brushed her hair from her face and then looked inside her nostrils. I wasn't quite sure what I was looking for, I just wanted to make sure she wasn't bleeding or anything. I kissed her lips while she grabbed my face in her hands. I knew at that moment that we might just be okay.

thirty

Tameka

I took the front passenger's seat on the way back to Atlanta as Sean maneuvered the SUV down I-20 headed east. We talked about everything under the sun as I tried to block thoughts of Vance from even entering my head. The beginning of the weekend had been an absolute nightmare as I busted up Vance's little dinner party with his girlfriend and her parents. And on top of all of it, he had the nerve to break up with me. It stung. I instantly felt like I was all alone in this world and pregnant. The last part of my weekend wasn't bad as I strolled through the mall with my girls and Sean, went to a frat party on Saturday night and even checked out a movie on Sunday.

Sean had stayed up until almost four o'clock in the morning listening to me spill my guts all over the place. We sat outside in Calvin's father's SUV listening to music and talking; that is, until both our eyes started to flutter and we decided that we needed to call it a night. Sean was sweet. He didn't even complain when I started to repeat myself through the night. He didn't roll his eyes up into his head when I cried—*four times*. He didn't even mind when I called Vance's voice mail at two-thirty and told him what a sorry loser he was, and a deadbeat dad. I used choice words that I knew I shouldn't have but I needed to get some things off my chest.

Sean just simply shook his head and asked, "You feel better?"

"A little," I'd told him, and then went on to the next phase of my emotional roller coaster.

Once we reached the Atlanta metro area, Sean stopped for one last fill-up. Everyone who had fallen asleep was now awake and groggy from the drive. As Sean drove slowly down Tymia's street, Mommy's car was the first one that I noticed. It was parked in the driveway behind Indigo's father's truck. Jade's mom's car was parked in front of the house. My heart started beating uncontrollably and I couldn't help but wonder what awaited us inside that house. Sean pulled up behind Jade's mom's car and we all just looked at each other.

"Oh my God, I will be on punishment for the rest of the summer!" Indigo exclaimed.

"You?" Jade was all bug-eyed as if she'd seen a ghost. "I don't even want to go in there."

"Tameka, do you think Aunt Mel will tell my parents about this?" Alyssa asked. "This could completely ruin my summer."

"I doubt if she'll tell," I told her, but she didn't seem convinced.

"I talked to my mama the other day and she didn't seem like she knew anything," Tymia said.

"Whew, I'm glad my mom's not here." Asia smiled.

"Don't get too happy," I told her. "Ain't that your mama on the front porch?"

She took a closer look at the woman in a yellow sundress standing on the porch yapping with someone on her cell phone.

"Ooh, that is her!" Asia said. "How did she get over here? Oh, there's her car." It was hidden on the other side of Indigo's dad's truck.

"Well, we might as well get on out...get this over with," I said and then opened the passenger's door.

"Tameka, wait!" Indi said. "I just need to breathe for a second."

"Shouldn't we like...come up with a story?" Jade asked.

"What story? They obviously know that we weren't at Tymia's house for the weekend. And they know that we weren't at any of the other houses. What is there to come up with besides the truth?" I asked.

"Yeah, you're probably right." Indi stuffed two pieces of gum into her mouth back-to-back.

"Give me one of those," Asia said. "Might soften the blow."

"Gum is gonna soften the blow?" I laughed. "Come on y'all, let's go."

"You're just so eager to go because you know that Mel is cool and you probably won't get any more than a scolding," Jade snapped. "But me...my mama don't play. Now my daddy's a pushover, but Mommy...she's a little crazy. She might actually swing on me."

"Well, nothing's gonna change if we sit here," I said.

"Okay, let's do this." Indigo exhaled and then opened her door.

She was the first to hop out. Sean and Calvin followed and opened the back hatch so that we could grab our bags. They handed over our loot but weren't trying to stick around for any length of time. Before stepping back into the car, Sean gave me a strong hug.

"Call me later if you're not on punishment," he said.

"Whatever." I laughed. "I can't remember the last time I was on punishment."

"Speak for yourself." Indigo threw the strap of her bag over her shoulder and headed for the house.

"I *am* speaking for myself," I said. "Sean, I will definitely call you later."

"Cool," he said before hopping into the car; he and Calvin pulled off in a hurry.

The six of us slowly made our way up Tymia's driveway. Asia's mother finished her call and then shut her phone.

"Asia Marie Jones, may I ask where the heck you've been for the weekend?" she asked.

"Huh?" Asia asked, dumbfounded.

"Don't 'huh' me," Miss Jones said.

"I would like to know the same thing!" Jade's mom, Barbara Morgan, stepped out onto the porch. "You already know that you're in trouble, right?"

"Told y'all she was crazy," Jade mumbled softly. "Yes, ma'am," she yelled to her mother.

We all made our way into the house, where Indigo's parents sat on the couch with cold glasses of lemonade in their hands. Mommy sat at the dining room table with Tymia's mother, flipping through a magazine, and Jade's father paced the floor.

Mommy looked up from her magazine and said, "Tameka, I can't even believe you would pull something like this. You're in no position to be on the road somewhere anyway."

"Where did y'all go?" Carolyn Summer asked. "Y'all had us worried sick!"

"We went to…um…we went to Grambling, Louisiana." I swallowed. Hard.

"Grambling, Louisiana?" Jade's father, Ernest Morgan, asked. "What in the world is in Grambling, Louisiana?"

All five pairs of eyes landed on me, as if it was all my idea that we trampled down to the little country town and they didn't have a say in the matter.

"Um…my friend Sean is thinking of going to college down there and so we went down there to check things out…look around." I don't know what made me glance over at Mommy. I waited for her to bust me out, to say, "Everybody's knows your little nappy-headed boyfriend Vance goes to school down there! You think you're slick, but you're not." But she didn't say any of that. She just gave me a look that said, "I'll deal with you when I get home…but right now, you're on your own. Let me see you weasel your way out of this one."

"I hope you're not considering going to Grambling, Indi," Carolyn Summer said. "You're going to Spelman. We've already talked about this. You can forget about going to school in that little country town."

"I second that," Barbara Morgan said. "Jade and Indigo have been planning to go to Spelman since they were in the seventh grade!"

Asia's mom gathered her purse onto her shoulder. "Come on here, Asia, we need to go. I've got errands to run and I need to have a word with you. Rita, thank you so much for dinner. It was wonderful."

"Yes, it was, and it was so good to spend some time with you. We have to make sure we keep the lines of communication open for these kids who think they slick. I guess they forgot that we used to be teenagers, too." Aunt Carolyn stood. "Come on, Harold, let's go."

Mr. Summer took his glass and Aunt Carolyn's to the kitchen. My mother didn't make a move. She just watched me from the dining room table. And even after Rita had said her goodbyes to all the parents and ushered everyone out the door, Mommy was still sitting there. Alyssa and I took a seat side by side on the sofa.

Tymia threw her bag over her shoulder. "I'll holler at y'all later," she whispered. "I'm avoiding the line of fire."

"All right, text me later, after you get your whipping." I smiled.

"Whatever," she said before disappearing up a flight of stairs.

Alyssa and I sat there for what seemed like forever before I finally interrupted my mother's and Ms. Rita's conversation. "Mommy, can we go now?" I asked, treading waters carefully.

"As soon as I'm done talking to Rita," she said. "Why don't you and Alyssa go on outside and put your stuff in the car. Here are the keys."

The two of us stood and I grabbed the keys from Mommy. Alyssa and I stepped out into the Atlanta heat, our bags in tow. I hit the power locks and we threw our bags into the trunk, sat in the car and waited for Mommy.

"I don't really know what's up," I told Alyssa as I changed the radio station from V-103 to 107.9. I started the car and turned on the air-conditioning. "They all over here having dinner together, when just a few days ago they barely even knew Tymia's mama."

"Well, they know her now," Alyssa said. "I saw my life flash before my eyes. If Aunt Mel tells my parents about this weekend, they'll probably cut my summer vacation short and send for me to come home. Not to mention, I'll be on punishment until school starts."

"Mommy's acting a little strange but I don't think she's going to sail you down the river."

Finally the front door opened and she appeared on the porch, still running her mouth with Ms. Rita. They said their goodbyes, even gave each other a hug, and then Mommy approached the car. She hopped into the driver's seat and slowly backed out of the driveway.

"So, Tameka Brown, how did you enjoy your weekend?" she asked, looking all cute in her brown top and matching lip color.

"What color is that lipstick, Chintz or Paramount?" I asked, trying to avoid the subject like the plague.

"Let's stick to one subject at a time, young lady. I'm disappointed in you, Tameka. I thought you were so much more responsible than what you displayed this weekend. What were you thinking, going out of town for the weekend and not telling me?"

"At the time it seemed like a pretty good idea. I'm sorry, Mommy."

"I don't give you any hassles about stuff, Tameka. I'm a pretty lenient mom, aren't I?"

"You are, and I wanted to tell you. I can't tell you how many times I wanted to call you...and say..."

"But you didn't. That's what's killing me. What if something happened to you or the baby? Then what, Tameka?"

I was silent. She was right.

"When Sean asked us if we wanted to go, I guess we just got caught up in the moment," I finally said.

"And because you all figured that since none of us really knew Rita, you could get away with telling us that you were spending the weekend over here," she said. "But your little plan backfired, didn't it? We all know Rita very well now. And all you girls did was bring us closer together, and from now on it'll be harder for you to get one over on any of us. Believe that."

I felt horrible. Mommy and I were best friends and I should've been able to tell her anything.

"I just wanted to check up on Vance and see what he was doing," I told her.

"Well, did you get a chance to see what he was doing?"

"I sure did." I glanced out the window. Suddenly I was back in that uncomfortable place again—at the restaurant where I'd made a complete fool of myself.

"And?" Mommy asked.

"And I ran into him and his new girlfriend. She's pretty, and skinny and not pregnant. I was so hurt, Mommy. I wanted to call you…to tell you. But I knew that if I called you and told you where I was, you would be placed in a bad position of having to tell all the other parents where we were."

"And you're right. I would've been forced to tell the other parents."

"Aunt Mel, you don't have to tell my parents if you don't want to," Alyssa said.

"Well, your case is a little different, young lady. You're in my care right now, so I'll just beat your behind myself instead of telling your parents."

"Sorry, Aunt Mel." She shut up, pulled her seat belt tighter and glanced out the window.

"Don't mention it," Mommy said, peeked into her rearview mirror at Alyssa and then glanced over at me. "So finish telling me."

I told her all about what happened with Vance. Even about the breakup. And after I'd spilled my guts, she said, "He called me. That's how I knew where you were."

"He called you?"

Vance was the one who had blown our cover? I wanted to strangle him. He just couldn't stop making my life miserable!

"Yes, Vance called me a few days ago. Told me all about everything that went down."

"He called you? Who did he think he was, calling you?"

"Someone who was concerned about you. He wanted to make sure that I knew where you were and that you were okay. He was concerned."

"Yeah, right. I doubt that. Did he tell you about his little girlfriend?"

"He mentioned a young lady, yes. I was really glad that he

called. Especially since you didn't have the good sense to call me yourself. You were so busy trying to protect your friends. And that's why I called every one of their parents. Told them what happened and that they should meet me over Rita's."

Suddenly Vance had become the hero in this situation and she didn't seem to care at all that I was really the victim here.

"So you knew all this time? Why didn't you call me?"

"What? And give you and your girlfriends a heads-up? So that you all could come up with a great scheme? Oh no…you forced me to do it this way. I had a responsibility to all the parents. Now, had you involved me from the beginning, I probably could've helped you out but you didn't handle this right."

"So now I guess I'm on punishment?"

"No, actually I think you've been punished enough," she said. "But, Tameka, I think you're missing the big picture. Do you know how huge this is? You are pregnant and sixteen! Do you know how dangerous it was for you to just take it upon yourself to leave the city limits without telling me?"

"I do understand. And I'm sorry. I learned my lesson."

Mommy glanced at me sideways. "I'm sorry that you had to go through that stuff with Vance." She grabbed my hand and held on to it.

"At least now I don't have to worry about what he's doing, right?"

"We'll get through this…together, baby. You know that, don't you?"

I shook my head yes and then glanced out the window. Suddenly it was depressing to think about going through this pregnancy alone, bringing my baby into a broken relationship. This was not how it was supposed to be. I thought about that night with Vance, the night he showed up at my door when my parents were gone. I had escorted him to my bedroom that night. Lloyd's "Love Making 101" playing softly in the background as we did everything that the song said we should. And now I was paying the price.

As Mommy turned into our subdivision, tears began to flow from my eyes. How did everything get so messed up?

thirty-one

Marcus

ı **held** on to the arms of my seat as the plane made its descent into Hartsfield-Jackson International Airport. I felt the wheels of the plane touch the runway with a thump as I peered out the little window and watched as we taxied to the gate. As soon as the plane came to a complete halt, I could hear the unsnapping of seat belts all over the plane. I touched the pocket of my jeans just to make sure that the little blue box was still there; a silver chain with the letter *I* dangling from it was inside. It was an inexpensive gift that I'd picked up at one of the shops at the Boston airport. It seemed perfect for Indigo.

I hoped to see her face within the next few minutes as she waited in the baggage claim area with my father. I hadn't talked to her personally because she was still ignoring my calls, but I had asked Pop to go next door and ask her to come along. I wasn't sure if she would be there but I hoped and prayed that she would.

As I took the long escalator up, adjusting the strap of my carry-on luggage, my heart started to pound. I couldn't wait to see Indigo's face; it had been a long summer without her and I missed her like crazy. I had messed up—I knew that.

But I hoped with my heart and soul that I could get her to forgive me. Once at the top of the escalator, I looked around—in search of my beautiful Indigo Summer. My eyes roamed rapidly around the airport at all the other strange faces, in search of one familiar one. I found a familiar face, but it wasn't Indigo's—it was Pop's.

"Hey there, son." He was all grins, dressed in a pair of oily coveralls and waving to me. Once I reached the top, he grabbed me into a warm embrace, despite the oil.

"Hey, Pop," I said and gave him a quick handshake. "Been working on your truck again?"

"Put a new alternator in it," he said. "Just in time to get here and pick you up. Barely had time to wash my hands."

"Thought you were bringing Indigo with you," I said.

"I went over there, asked her if she wanted to come. Said she had something else to do," he said nonchalantly. "Guess you'll have to catch up with her later."

My stomach felt as if someone had just punched me in it. I guessed that whatever Indigo was dishing out at this point, I deserved it.

"Guess I will," I told Pop as we made our way over to the carousel to pick up the rest of my luggage. "Did she say what she had to do?"

"Nah, son, she didn't gimme any details. Just said she had something else to do. Matter of fact, I think she was on punishment anyhow. Something about her and her little girlfriends sneaking down to Grambling, Louisiana, for the weekend. Harold and Carolyn weren't too happy about that at all."

"Grambling, Louisiana?"

"Yeah, I didn't get many details from Harold when he came over and had a beer the other day."

My heart rejoiced—just a little. That was it! That was why she wasn't answering or returning my calls. And that was why she hadn't come to the airport. She was grounded. Probably had gone to Grambling with her friend Tameka whose boyfriend attended school there. It didn't surprise me one bit that their little diva squad had come up with one of their schemes—a scheme that they obviously hadn't thought through, because they got caught. Whatever the case, I felt better.

"So she probably couldn't come to the airport anyway," I said to Pop.

"Well, Harold said that she could come along if she wanted to. She just didn't want to."

My celebration ended quickly and that punch-in-the-stomach feeling was back again. He could've saved that comment. *She just didn't want to.* Those words rang in my head all the way home. What if I really had lost Indigo forever this time? What if she had moved on, found someone else? It was true that she'd visited Grambling for the weekend. She was a beautiful girl. It would only take a hot second for someone to notice her, push up on her and steal her away. Maybe she had already kissed him, exchanged numbers with him, and they were sending text messages back and forth to each other at this very moment. Maybe he was making her smile, telling her how beautiful she was. Maybe he was telling her that she had the dumbest boyfriend in the whole world because he had let her slip through his fingers.

"Did you hear me, son?" Pop was asking.

"What'd you say?" I hadn't heard a thing my father was saying. I was too busy letting my thoughts take me to another place, a place I didn't really want to be.

"I said, are you hungry?" he repeated.

"Nah, I'm good. I had a burger at the airport in Boston. I just want to get to the house," I told him. I wanted to get to

Indigo as soon as humanly possible. Break up her little text messaging party with her new boyfriend. I wouldn't let her go without a fight.

I had hoped that she would be sitting outside on her front porch when we pulled up but she wasn't. I hopped out of the truck, grabbed my bags out of the back and rushed inside. I rushed upstairs to my room, lifted the window, pulled a package of candy out of my overnight bag and threw a few of them at Indigo's window. My heart skipped a beat when her face appeared in the window; even with the frown, it was still beautiful. Her hair was a wild mass on her head as if she'd been sleeping.

She lifted the window and stood there with her hand on her hips. "Yes?"

"What's up, girl? I'm back in the A-T-L!" I tried to sound as if nothing had happened between us. As if my lips hadn't been against Daria's less than two weeks prior. "Aren't you going to welcome me back?"

"Welcome back," she stated dryly.

"I'm glad to see you." I smiled. Hoped for a smile from her. She didn't give me one. "Can I see you for a minute. At the creek?"

The creek was where Indigo and I would meet from time to time. It's where serious conversations took place, where we had our first kiss. It's where I asked her to be my girl for the very first time. Lots of firsts at that creek. I knew that I needed to win her heart back, and what better place than that?

"Can't," she said.

"Why not?"

"Got chores."

"It won't take long," I promised.

She sighed. She was playing hard, and I realized that it

wasn't going to be as easy as I thought. But I knew that if I could get her back there, she would give in. She had to. I needed her to.

"Gimme five minutes. I just woke up," she said and then slammed her window shut and disappeared. She was being rude but I didn't care. I just needed to see her, hold her in my arms. I needed her like I needed fresh air.

At the creek, I sat on a huge rock and tossed smaller rocks into the water. I couldn't wait to see Indigo, up close and personal. I wondered what she would be wearing, wondered if she'd changed any since I left for Harvard. I'd changed. Not physically but definitely mentally. I'd grown up over the summer. I knew that I'd taken Indigo for granted and that the grass is not always greener somewhere else. I used to hear my parents use that phrase, but never really understood it until now. I knew that whatever pretty girls were out there in the world, none of them could compare to the one I had—or used to have.

When I heard the light rustling of her flip-flops amongst the leaves, I turned to face her. She wore a red tank top and a pair of denim shorts. She'd tried to tame her hair by pulling it into a ponytail but it didn't help much. Her face was a little red from being sunburned. Her lips were shiny from the lip gloss that she'd obviously just rubbed on. They looked kissable, and if I played my cards right I'd be kissing them soon.

"You look cute." I smiled.

"Thanks."

"Heard you and your girls got in trouble for going down to Grambling without permission."

"Yeah, the whole trip was a nightmare."

"What were y'all thinking?"

"Tameka's friend Sean was going down there to hang out

with his cousin, so he invited us along. None of our parents really knew Tymia's mother so she was our perfect alibi. We all said that we were spending the night at Tymia's house, hoping that none of our parents would find out the truth."

"How did they find out?"

"It all started when Tameka and Vance broke up," she said.

"What? Tameka and Vance broke up?"

"Yeah. She busted up on him with another girl having dinner at this stupid fancy restaurant. The girl claimed to be Vance's girlfriend, but when Tameka waddled into the restaurant, stomach and all, the girl started trippin'…long story short, Vance called Mel to let her know that he broke up with Tameka and to make sure she was all right…."

"So was she all right?" I asked. I knew that Indigo's friend Tameka really cared about Vance Armstrong. But I also knew that Vance was a ladies' man and wasn't the type to settle down with one girl. Tameka was sixteen and pregnant, and I knew that Vance would bolt one day. I just didn't expect it so soon.

"She's dealing with it."

"Are you all right, Indi?" I asked her. Indigo had been hurt, too—by me. Knowing that was tearing my heart apart.

"I'm dealing with it."

I reached for her hand and she pulled it away.

"I'm so sorry, Indi. I don't really know how to make it up to you. I know I can't change what happened, but I know that I don't want to lose you. I'll do whatever it takes to win your heart back."

"You hurt me too bad, Marcus. I don't know if I wanna do this anymore."

"Are you for real?"

"I'm for real, Marcus. I can't believe you were down there kissing all up on another girl. I don't know what she got!

And then you think you gon' kiss me again? I don't think so!" She said, "Nah, I think we just need to step back for a little while."

My heart dropped to the ground when she said that. I didn't really know where to take the conversation from there. The last thing I wanted to do was *step back for a little while,* as Indigo suggested. I decided to lighten the conversation a bit, charm her with my humor. I rushed toward her and grabbed her around the waist. She didn't pull away this time and I was glad.

"What you mean I can't kiss you again, girl?" I whispered.

"I don't know where your lips have been, Marcus. And I definitely don't know where hers have been, either."

I pulled Indigo even closer, brushed my lips softly against her cheek and then her earlobe. "You know you wanna kiss me, girl...trying to play hard to get."

"I don't wanna kiss you," she said it with attitude, but her lips were saying something different because she didn't pull them away when I kissed her.

I held on to her for dear life. Didn't want to let her go.

"I brought you something," I said and then dug into my pocket for the little blue box. I pulled it out and handed it to Indigo.

She opened it and then held the chain into the air. "It's pretty. Thank you, Marcus. Is this a guilt gift?"

"It's just a gift to say that I love you and missed you."

"Cool. Put it around my neck."

I secured the clasp around Indigo's neck and watched the charm dangle in the middle of her chest. It looked good there. As I kissed her lips one last time, I hoped that through all of this, we could recover from the aftermath of a girl named Daria Charles.

thirty-two

Tameka
A week before Thanksgiving...

MY greatest fear: walking through the halls of my high school for the first time with my stomach the size of a watermelon. The first week had been worse than I imagined. And even though it had been months since school first started, people still stood with their lockers opened as I passed, staring, some of them whispering. I was a spectacle and it hurt. It hurt worse than the time I fell on the playground and ripped a huge hole in the knee of my white tights. I had to walk around like that for the remainder of the day with a bloody knee. And it was worse than that time I had the hickey on my forehead from running into a tree, or the time I got my period right in the middle of World History and messed up my lime-green capris. This had to be far worse than anything I'd ever been through.

There were other pregnant girls at my school—Tasha Hunter was pregnant, Rita Young and Missy Collier. It was nothing new to see girls my age waddling through the halls, but everyone seemed to zero in on me; as if I was the only one on the face of the earth who'd made a mistake. I kept my eyes straight; tried not to look at anyone as I made the way to my locker. I put in the combination—22 left, 10 right, 25 left. Tried opening it, nothing. I put the combination in again—22 left, 10 right, 25 left. Nothing. All I wanted to do was grab my books and rush to my class.

"Sometimes you have to jiggle the lock a little bit," Rita Young said as she approached. Her stomach looked as if it might pop at any minute. She jiggled the lock and opened my locker. "See?"

"Thanks," I said. "It sticks sometimes."

"I didn't know you were pregnant, too. How many months are you?"

"Nine," I said. "I'm due the day after Thanksgiving but I'm praying that it's sooner."

"I'm due on Friday." Rita giggled and rubbed her belly. "But it can be any day now."

"Thanks for helping me with my locker." I smiled.

"No problem," she said. "And don't let the folks around here intimidate you. You made a mistake. So what? At least you're still here trying to get your education. Just ignore the stares and the whispers. They don't know what it's like."

"I'll try."

"Who's your baby's father?"

"Vance Armstrong."

"Oh, I remember him. He played ball," she said. "Didn't he graduate last year?"

"Yep, went away to college," I said, "and we broke up over the summer."

"At least he's still alive, though. Not like my baby's daddy who was murdered. He was involved in a gang and some fools shot him. Just shot him in cold blood and left him for dead."

"I'm sorry to hear that."

"My baby is all I have left of him. And since my parents

kicked me out when they found out I was pregnant, I been trying to do this on my own."

"Who's gonna help you raise the baby?"

She shrugged her shoulders. "Just me."

The more I talked to Rita, the smaller my problems became. I had parents who loved me, and Vance's parents had promised to help with the baby's expenses. Although Vance and I had broken up, he promised that he would still be there for the baby. At least I had support. Rita didn't have anything. I watched as she waddled down the hall and went into her classroom. I grabbed my books and slammed my locker shut and went to my first class.

"Where have you been all day?" Indigo and the girls found me right before lunch. "I've been looking for you all day!"

"Keeping a low profile," I told her.

"A low profile?" Tymia chimed in.

"Whatever!" Asia said. "You can't hide from us, girl-friend. Not with a stomach like that!"

"Now that we found this hoochie, can we go eat lunch, please?" said Jade. "I am starving."

"I'm not going to lunch," I announced.

"What?" they all said in unison.

"I'm not going to lunch," I repeated. "Not hungry."

"Are you crazy?" Indigo asked and placed her hand on my belly. "You have to feed this child."

"And besides, lunch is our time to hang out."

"I don't wanna hang out."

"Tameka, look…you're not the only pregnant girl at this school. Nobody cares," Indigo stated. She had no idea how hard it was just to walk down the hall. With her skinny little body, she didn't know what it was like to be in my state.

"You don't see the looks that I get from people...the whispers and the stares."

"Screw them!" Jade said, and then glared at two girls who were walking past, staring. "Who are they to judge you?"

"She's right, Tameka," Asia said. "Everybody makes mistakes."

"Any girl that's having sex can end up pregnant. Condoms aren't a hundred percent effective and neither are birth control pills," Indigo said. "Now come on. I know this food ain't Burger King or nothing, but at least it'll hit the spot."

Indigo grabbed my arm and led me to the cafeteria. The days were becoming harder to bear and I wondered what the days that followed would be like.

With toilet paper in between my toes and a fruit smoothie in my hand, I reclined on my bed while Indigo painted my toenails hot pink. I had just painted hers lime green, while Tymia painted Asia's tangerine and Jade painted Alyssa's bright red.

In just a short time I had managed to stop thinking about Vance every minute of the day. I was at a place where I only thought of him every now and then. And even those times didn't last very long. He'd called a few times, just to see how I was doing and to make sure that his parents were still sending money for the baby. And they were. His mother had already purchased a crib, a car seat and several boxes of diapers. She'd brought over undershirts, onesies and lots of little pink and purple socks.

Becoming a mom was becoming more and more real each day. It was becoming a little scary because it was something very new and different for me. I'd never been anybody's mama before and the thought of it had me nervous. When I thought about all the stuff Mommy had done for me and how she and Daddy raised me, I wondered if I could do the same for my baby. It was even scarier to think about having to do it all alone. I knew I'd be okay, though. At least I had my parents and my friends.

"Okay, chica, I'm done with your pink toes." Indigo closed the bottle of fingernail polish. "Now you can do my fingernails."

Indigo rested the palm of her hand on my knee while I painted her fingernails lime green to match her toes.

"So what's up with you and Marcus? You gon' stop being stubborn and grant that boy some forgiveness?"

She shrugged.

"She know she's in love with Marcus Carter," Jade said. "I don't know why she's playing all hard. He gave her that silver chain that she's been sporting around her neck since he came back from Harvard. She wouldn't be wearing it if she didn't still love the boy."

"Nobody said I didn't love still love him," Indigo defended herself. "I'm just mad at him right now."

"He obviously didn't care anything about that girl in Boston, or he wouldn't be running around here moping and begging for your forgiveness," Tymia offered.

"Marcus is still a good dude," I had to say. "He just messed up."

"Yeah," Asia added. "Wasn't it your idea two summers ago to have that stupid pact…break up for the summer just in case you bumped into someone else?"

"Yeah, but there was no pact in place when Marcus went away this past summer. He just took it upon himself to hook up with somebody else," she said. "And I'll forgive him when I'm good and ready."

"Okay, *good and ready*. You wait too long and somebody else is going to scoop that fine brother up," Jade said.

When Indigo's ringtone filled the air, everybody looked her way as she stared at the screen. We all knew who it was as she pressed the button and mumbled, "I'm on my way out," and then hung up.

"Who was that?" I smiled.

"Nobody!" She pulled her nails away, started blowing them dry. "I'll be right back."

"Where you going?" Jade asked.

"Marcus is out front." She grinned. "I'm just gonna go and say hi."

We all burst out in laughter as Indigo opened my bedroom door, rushed down the stairs and out front to meet Marcus. She wasn't fooling any of us. She still loved him and, in her heart, she had already forgiven him. Marcus was a great guy despite his mistake and Indigo knew it. Indigo and Marcus was one of those couples that you wanted to see together forever and ever. It wouldn't be right for them to break up because they belonged together.

As I sat in the middle of my bed, I rubbed my stomach. I knew that I had a long road ahead of me. But I had already made up in my mind that I was going to be brave. I knew it wasn't going to be easy but I would be a champion. When I walked the halls of Carver High, I would ignore all the stares and whispers that were sure to come. It was only important that I finished high school and gave birth to a healthy baby. Nothing else mattered but those two things. Everything else would take a backseat.

When Lil Wayne's voice rushed through the speakers, I stood up and started moving my hips to the music. All my girls did the same and before long we were singing along, too. My life was changing. My body was different. My world had already turned upside down and then right side up again. And I was sure that it would continue to be topsy-turvy for just a little while longer. I was different, more mature than I had ever been at. And I wasn't done growing—both mentally and physically. But in spite of everything that had gone on, I knew that there was nothing I couldn't handle.

As the music filled my room, I looked around as my friends got lost in the music. I knew that they had my back for the long haul. And I would definitely need them. My road was unpaved and sure to be bumpy. As they all danced to the music, I decided to just watch them. Placing my palm on my stomach, I smiled. Let the music take me away. There was something about Lil Wayne's voice that could set a party off right.

thirty-three

Marcus

senior year had finally arrived, and my days had been spent tying up loose ends and preparing for graduation—taking SATs and senior photos and ordering my cap and gown for graduation. Because I had enough credits, I was able to graduate early. I would attend my senior prom and graduate with the rest of my class, but I wouldn't have to attend classes anymore after December. Instead, I would spend second semester working as an intern at a law firm in downtown Atlanta. I was excited about that.

I looked forward to senior prom. Of course, I would probably take Indigo—that is, if we were still together. She was acting all hard, as if she was still mad about Daria. But I was pretty sure she might forgive me soon, especially since Christmas was just around the corner. Girls loved Christmas gifts and Indigo was no different. But before we could think about senior prom, or even Christmas for that matter, we had to make it through Thanksgiving.

My family had been invited to Indigo's house for Thanksgiving. Her grandmother, Nana Summer, was coming in town for the holidays, which was a special treat for everyone who knew her. I loved Nana Summer, loved her like she was my own grandmother, and couldn't wait to see her. We had a lot to catch up on. I would tell her all about my summer visit to Harvard and how I messed up with Indi. She would know just what I should do and how to handle her stubborn granddaughter. Nana Summer would be my saving grace.

As I strolled through the halls and to my locker, I grinned. It wouldn't be long before this place was history. Although I would miss my friends, some of my teachers and all of my coaches, I knew that I was headed for a bright future. And I was ready for the world. I reached into my locker, grabbed my Algebra book and then slammed my locker shut. I stood for a moment, watching as Indigo passed by with her girls. She looked my way, and then stopped and came over.

"What's up?" she asked.

"Nothing."

"Why you just standing here then?"

"Just watching you," I said. "Can I walk you to class?"

She shrugged. "I guess."

Indigo led the way to her American History class, which was only a short distance down the hall.

"So why you still acting funny? You gonna act like this for the entire school year? You know I'll be graduating soon and you won't get to see me at school every day."

"I'm not acting funny, Marcus."

"Oh really? Is that why we're not sharing lockers this year and you don't wait for me after dance practice anymore? You don't even wait for me in between classes, either."

"You're tripping."

"Indi, I got a lot of stuff on my head right now. With school and graduation and stuff, I don't have a lot of time to play around. If you can't get past this thing with Daria, then maybe you should just..."

"Just what, Marcus? Break up with you? Is that what you want?"

"No, that's not what I want. But I really need you to have my back right now. I need you to either be my girl—or not. I can't handle the in-between stuff." I had to be straight up with her, even if I risked losing her.

"I gotta go, Marcus. The bell is about to ring, and I can't be late for class. I'll get a detention," she said, leaving my questions unanswered. "I'll see you after practice today. I'll wait for you."

"Cool," I mumbled and then jogged to my class.

Indigo needed to make up her mind—*and fast*.

After practice I waited around for Indigo to show up as she'd promised. With the strap of my gym bag on my shoulder, I stood with my back against the wall. Indigo's girls passed by—Jade, Tymia and Asia.

"What's up, Marcus?" Jade asked.

"You waitin' for Indi?" asked Asia.

"Yeah, where is she?"

"She left a long time ago. Tameka's mom called. She went into labor and they rushed her to the hospital," Tymia said. "We're headed over there now. You wanna come?"

"Who's driving?" I asked. I knew that none of them had driver's licenses.

"You are." Jade grinned, and then locked arms with me. Asia pulled on my other arm.

"I wasn't really going that way," I explained. Watching a girl in labor was not the type of evening I had in mind. "And besides, I got homework."

"Oh come on, Marcus! We wanna get there before she has the baby," Tymia said. "If we hurry, we can make it."

There wasn't any use fighting with them, so I gave in—led the way to my Jeep and the four of us hopped in. I popped in a Jay-Z CD and turned it up. It would be a long drive the hospital but at least Indigo would be there. As of late, it seemed that spending time with her was all that mattered.

thirty-four

Vance

AS I merged onto I-20 headed east toward Atlanta, I was flooded by a pool of emotions. It had only been a few hours since I'd received a call from my mother—excitement all in her voice because Tameka had gone into labor. I was already headed home for Thanksgiving. With Jaylen in the passenger's seat of my car, asleep with his head against the window and mouth wide open, I had plenty of alone time. The first hour, I pumped the music up as loud as I could get it, tried to drown my thoughts. Didn't want to think about the reality of what awaited me in Atlanta. In Grambling, I was a college student who played college ball and had a girlfriend who I studied with every night. I had a normal life filled with difficult classes, basketball practice and frat parties. When I arrived in Atlanta, my life would instantly change. I would be a father and my parents would be grandparents. My sister Lori would be somebody's aunt. The first hour of the drive, my heart pounded so rapidly, I thought I was having an anxiety attack.

Soon I decided to turn down the music; think things through like a man. There was a baby who was coming soon, and would need me. She would be small and weak, and wouldn't be able to do anything on her own. I wondered what the baby would look like; wondered if she would have my eyes or my funny-shaped ears. I hoped not. I hated my ears and hoped that the baby would inherit Tameka's ears instead—and her smile. She had a beautiful smile. And she had that cute little dimple in her cheek when she laughed.

I hoped that Tameka was okay. Hoped that she wasn't in too much pain. I'd heard that childbirth was the worst pain ever and that sometimes women died during childbirth. Even though I was sure that Tameka hated me, I hoped that she wasn't in much pain. I felt guilty for not telling Lexi that Tameka was in labor; the next time she saw me, I would be a father. *I would be a father.* Those words lingered in my head and wouldn't go away. They scared me, but at the same time they gave me joy. I smiled to myself and then glanced over at Jaylen, who was snoring louder than the music. Wanted to make sure he hadn't witnessed the smile on my face. He would think I was crazy. There was also a smile in my heart and I wasn't sure why it was there. But I knew I wouldn't be able to relax until I made it to the hospital.

After I hopped onto 285 headed south, I knew that I was almost there. Jaylen was finally starting to move around in his seat. His eyes popped open.

"Where are we?"

"Close to home," I said. "I'm headed straight for the hospital."

"Did she have the baby yet?"

"Not yet. My mom said that she's still in labor."

"Wow, it's been hours. How long does it take to pop a baby out?" Jaylen asked and then straightened in his seat.

"My mom said that first babies take a long time," I explained. "I can drop you off at your house if you want me to."

"Nah, I'm good. I with you, bro...for as long as it take.

At least until I get hungry. Then I got to find my mama's kitchen. I have missed her cooking like crazy."

"Same here. Nothing like my mom's cooking."

As I pulled into the hospital's parking garage, my heart started pounding again. I was glad that Jaylen wasn't aware of my emotional roller coaster. On the outside, I was cool and calm, but inside I was going crazy and fear was about to overtake me. I stepped out of the car, threw my leather jacket on and zipped it up. Jaylen and I stepped into the hospital lobby and looked around for a minute.

"Which floor?" Jaylen asked.

"I don't know. I guess the floor where babies are born."

Jaylen found an information desk and approached the blond woman who sat behind it. "Can you tell me which floor babies are born on?" he asked.

"That would be the maternity ward." The woman smiled. "Third floor."

"Thank you," Jaylen said and, grabbing the elbow of my jacket, led the way to the elevators. I was glad, too, because suddenly my legs were stiff. He called for the elevator and once it arrived, I stood there. Couldn't move.

"You coming?" he asked, stepping inside.

I knew that Jaylen had said something but I wasn't sure what. "What's wrong with you, man? We're going up...to the third floor...you know, the maternity ward."

He pulled me onto the elevator and pressed the button for the third floor. When the doors opened, I spotted a pregnant girl wearing a plush pink robe and strolling through the halls. She couldn't have been more than sixteen and I wondered if her baby's father was around, and if he was just as scared as I was. With her belly protruding, she struggled just to take a few steps. I wondered why she was wandering aimlessly through the halls instead of relaxing in a hospital bed with her feet in the air.

"You're doing good, Jasmine," said a nurse who passed by dressed in scrubs. "Keep walking…just a little bit more and you'll be ready soon."

You'll be ready soon? Ready for what?

"Vance!" My mother rushed toward me. "I'm so glad you're here. She's in there! They're prepping her."

"You mean the baby's about to come?" I asked as I hugged my mother.

"Yes, she is." Mom smiled, and then hugged Jaylen. "I'm so glad you both made it. She's fully dilated."

"What does that mean?" I asked.

"It means she's about to give birth at any moment," Mom said. "Come on. She's been asking for you. She wants you in the delivery room. But you have to hurry so you can get cleaned up."

"Whoa…" I stopped in my tracks. "The delivery room? I don't know about that, Ma. I don't know if I'm ready for all that."

"What do you mean? This is your child coming into this world, son. Don't you want to witness it?"

I suddenly felt hot and it seemed that I was sweating uncontrollably.

"I think I'll just find the waiting room…you know, where all the other dads are."

"At least come in and say hello to Tameka. Let her know you're here."

Reluctantly, I followed my mother down the long hallway and into a room where Tameka was reclining on a bed and her mother was holding her hand. Tameka's eyes were closed and her face frowned; she was breathing heavily through her lips.

Her mother, Mel, smiled at me as I entered the room. "She's having a contraction," she whispered.

After the contraction was over, Tameka opened her eyes and looked at me with tears in them. I gave her a smile, hoped that it would ease her fears.

"Hey," I said with a cracked voice.

"Hey," Tameka said.

"Vance, you can take over from here." Mel stood and my heart started pounding again. "All you have to do is hold her hand and help her through the pain."

"You'll be just fine, baby," my mother said and then she and Mel left the room.

Left me to do this alone. Didn't they know we were just kids? I had no idea what I was supposed to do or say—or not do or say. I approached the chair next to Tameka's bed, took a seat, grabbed her hand and intertwined her fingers with mine. No words were spoken between us but it felt as if we were on the same team and moving in the same direction.

thirty-five

Tameka

The best part of the day was when Vance walked into my room and grabbed my hand. Even though I was in pain, I managed a smile. I was so happy to see him. He seemed so nervous, and so was I. But at least we were nervous together. With each contraction, I squeezed Vance's hand and he caressed my arm. I was ready for the labor to end. I was ready for my baby to be born.

"So how's school going?" I asked Vance, just to break the ice.

"It's cool. College is a lot of work," he said. "What about you? Was it really bad when you went to school on the first day…being pregnant and all?"

"Yeah, it was pretty bad the first week. But after that, people got used to seeing me and I wasn't so much a freak anymore."

"You think you'll be able to get back on the dance team after you have the baby?" he asked.

"I hope so."

"That's cool."

Small talk with Vance helped me through some of the contractions, helped take my mind off of them. But when the pains started coming every second, the small talk became irritating and I just wanted Vance to shut up. I didn't quite remember when Dr. Franklin rushed into the room, but he was suddenly giving me instructions, telling me to push the baby out. I pushed with all my might. Pushed until Dr. Franklin said he could see the baby's head.

"You're doing fine, Tameka," he said. "Now just relax for a minute and I'll tell you when to push again."

It wasn't long before he was telling me to push. Push. Relax. Push. Relax. It was exhausting. But shortly after that, he held a pale little girl into the air and all the pushing didn't seem to matter anymore. She was so tiny and beautiful and I couldn't stop staring at her. I couldn't even remember the pain. It was a blur to me. I was too curious about the little girl who was screaming at the top of her lungs.

"It's a girl." Dr. Franklin smiled.

I already knew that. I'd had a sonogram done months before. He didn't seem to mind that it was a girl. In fact, after the nurse cleaned her up and wrapped her in a warm blanket, Vance held the little bundle in his arms and stared at her as if she wasn't real.

"What's her name gonna be?"

"Maybe Vanessa," I said. It was a name that I'd chosen months before because it began with the same letter as Vance's name. "Vanessa Dionne."

"Vanessa Dionne Armstrong," Vance added. "I like that."

He grabbed her small hand and wrapped it around his pinkie finger.

"Give her here and go tell everybody to come and see her."

Vance gently placed Vanessa into my arms and then smiled. "She's so...dang, she's so little...and cute."

"Yep, she is cute, huh? Kind of like her mama." I grinned.

"She looks just like you," he said and then left the room. That was the best moment ever.

* * *

My parents rushed into the room, followed by Vance's parents and his little sister. A few minutes later, Indigo, Jade, Asia, Tymia and even Marcus came in to see the baby. Mommy and Mrs. Armstrong seemed to fight over who would hold her next. When Indigo finally got her turn, Marcus stood over her—both of them admiring little Vanessa. After Indigo passed Vanessa on to Jade, she reached for Marcus's hand and I knew that they must've finally squashed their differences. At least I hoped so. Marcus was a great guy. At least she had someone who loved her and wanted her.

As I glanced over at Vance, who was finally holding his daughter again, I suddenly remembered that he belonged to someone else. Soon the newness of the baby would wear off and Thanksgiving would be over and Vance would be headed for Grambling again—and into the arms of the girl that had stolen his heart from me in the first place. I knew that whatever moment we were sharing would be short-lived. I didn't care. I would remember this day for the rest of my life.

After all the excitement died down and everybody went home, I managed to finally doze off. I was awakened in the middle of the night by Nurse Liz, the night nurse who had been assigned to care for the baby and me. She was holding Vanessa in her arms.

"Hello, Miss Tameka. Little Vanessa is hungry. Would you like to feed her?"

I would like to get some sleep…finish the awesome dream I was having! It was about Vance and me. He'd finally come to his senses and dumped that girl at Grambling. We were getting married—I had on a beautiful white dress and my hair was styled in a bunch of curls. I had on a pair of strappy heels that I'd seen at the mall. And Indigo, Jade, Asia and Tymia were my bridesmaids. They were dressed in purple gowns. It was so real.

"I'm sorry, I was sleeping," I said. "Can't you just give her a bottle?"

"Well, it's always good for the new mothers to feed their own babies…get used to doing it. When you take her home, you'll have to do this, honey."

I didn't have the strength to fight it. I just grabbed Vanessa in my arms and took the warm bottle from Nurse Liz's fingers. It was still awkward holding the baby, but I knew I needed the practice. Mommy told me that I needed to secure her neck and head. I did that and then stuck the nipple of the bottle into her mouth. Her eyes were bright— she was wide awake at three o'clock in the morning! How could someone so small have so much energy at this hour? It was scary. Was she planning to be awake every morning at three o'clock?

"I'll come back to check on you in a little bit," Nurse Liz said and then stepped out of the room.

I was nervous to be alone with the baby. What if I messed up? It was hard to believe that this little person belonged to me—I was responsible for her. I would have to feed her and change her diapers. I'd rock her to sleep in the middle of the night and play with her tiny fingers and toes. I would have to make decisions about her life and take her to see the doctor. She was mine. All mine.

After Vanessa's feeding, I rocked her to sleep. Soon, Nurse Liz came back for her and I was able to get some sleep. I was grateful for sleep because I was plenty tired. When I woke up, the sun was beaming through my window. I managed to sit up in the bed and when I glanced across the room, Vance was asleep in the orange chair near the door. I watched him for a moment. Wondered how long he'd been sitting there.

"Hey," he said once his eyes popped open.

"Hey. I didn't know you were here. How long have you been here?"

"About an hour. You were sleeping so hard, I didn't want to wake you," he said. "I just came by to see Vanessa. I saw her in the nursery. She was knocked out, just like you."

"Well, I guess so. We both had a long night. She was up at three and I had to feed her."

"Three o'clock in the morning?"

"Yep," I told him. "And it's almost time for her feeding again. You wanna feed her this time?"

"I don't know. She's so…you know…tiny."

"You just have to hold her carefully. That's all."

I picked up the remote control that was attached to my bed, started surfing the channels until I found MTV. Somebody was having a DNA test done to find out if her fiancé was the father of her baby. Turned out, he wasn't. She started screaming and crying and ran offstage. Her fiancé covered his face with the palms of his hands. He was hurt. I wondered if Vance believed that Vanessa was his or if I'd have to find my way to the show and have a DNA test done, too. I wondered if he was going to flake out on me and disappear. I wondered if he would still want to see Vanessa after he made it back to Grambling. I wondered if he would call or write and come home for her birthdays. So many unanswered questions.

"Vanessa has my nose," Vance stated. "And her fingers are long and skinny like mine. My mom said she has piano fingers."

"Yeah, her fingers are long and skinny."

"Maybe she'll play ball like me," he said.

"I doubt that." I laughed. "She'll probably be a dancer."

Vance and I laughed and talked like old times—two parents planning our child's future. I remembered how much I missed him. Wished things could be the way they were before Grambling. There was a time when we had so many plans for our future. We couldn't stop talking to each other. It was as if we had to cram a year's worth of conversation into one morning. I barely even heard his phone ring. I hoped that he would silence it, particularly since he wasn't supposed to be talking on it in the hospital. But he didn't silence it, he answered.

"Hello," he said. "Hey you, what's up? Yeah, I miss you, too…"

I miss you, too. It was as if my heart stopped beating. It had to be his girlfriend on the other end of the phone.

"…I know. I'm at the hospital right now…seeing Vanessa…"

Seeing Vanessa? If he's here to see Vanessa, then why is he all up in my room watching TV?

"…Okay, I'll call you later…yeah, me, too…"

Did she say that she loved him?

He hung up, looked my way. "Sorry about that."

"You're not supposed to have cell phones in here," I explained.

My mood was different. Once again, a girl named Lexi had stolen my joy. Nurse Liz walked in with Vanessa and a warm bottle and I was grateful. Things were suddenly awkward and we needed to change the atmosphere.

"He's gonna feed her." I volunteered Vance before he had a chance to protest.

Nurse Liz placed Vanessa in Vance's arms and smiled. "Here you go."

He adjusted her until he found a perfect fit. Her head relaxed against his arm and he stuck the nipple of the bottle into her mouth. I watched the two of them. Wished I had my digital camera so I could capture the moment and remember it forever. Instead I burned it into my memory and hoped that it stayed there. I guess in life, you held on to the precious moments—even if they were short-lived.

thirty–six

Marcus

Nana's cornbread dressing had to be the highlight of Thanksgiving, and we won't even discuss the macaroni and cheese and collard greens. I ate more than I should have and decided to find a corner spot in the family room to recover. With football on the television and light jazz floating through the house, the Summers' house was filled with joy. The men drank beers and watched the game and yelled each time something exciting happened. The women chitchatted and giggled in the formal living room, while Indigo and her girls gathered upstairs in her bedroom—with the door shut. Lord only knew what they were discussing.

With a magazine in her hand, Nana slid next to me onto the sofa. "You ate too much, huh?"

"Everything was so good, Nana. I couldn't help it," I said. "I love Thanksgiving."

"You'll be leaving us soon…going away to college. I'm proud of you." Nana flipped through the pages of the magazine.

"Thank you."

"I always knew that you would do something spectacular." She grinned. "What are you going to do about that little girl upstairs?"

"I really don't know, Nana. I've been thinking a lot about it. I love her but I know I'll be leaving soon. I don't wanna tie her down."

"You both are young. You have your whole lives ahead of you," Nana said. "It's healthy to allow each other space to grow...to live."

"So you think we should break up?"

"I never said that."

"So you think we should try to make it work even though we'll be miles apart?"

"I never said that, either."

"Well, Nana, I don't know what to do."

"Son, when the time comes, you'll know exactly what to do." She patted my leg. "Now come on in the kitchen. Let's get us some dessert."

"Aw, Nana, I don't have any room for dessert." My stomach was at its fullest capacity.

"Oh, you have to taste Nana's sweet potato pie, boy. That's not an option. Now come on." Nana grabbed my hand, pulled me up from the sofa and led the way to the kitchen.

As I stood near the sink and ate a slice of pie, Indigo and her girls came into the kitchen.

"We're bored," Indi announced.

"How could you be bored when all your friends are here?" Nana asked.

"We've gossiped about everything we could possibly think about. There's no one else to drag through the mud." Indigo and her girls giggled as she turned on the kitchen radio.

"Cupid Shuffle" rang through the small speakers and Indigo began to bounce to the music. Jade followed and soon Asia and Tymia were moving, too.

"Come on, Nana," Asia said, "it's easy."

"Nana don't move quite like she used to." Nana laughed. "These old bones…"

"Aw, come on, Nana. You don't have to move that much," said Indigo.

"To the right, to the right, to the right, to the right," said Jade, showing Nana the moves.

"To the left, to the left, to the left, to the left," Asia said as Nana began to learn the steps.

"Now walk it by yourself," Tymia said.

It was funny watching Nana attempt to walk it out. Even though she didn't have all the moves, she gave it her best. After watching them for a moment, I decided to take a seat at the kitchen table and finish my sweet potato pie. Indigo looked good in her jeans and sweater, and the chain that I had given her dangled from her neck. She had always been the girl of my dreams, with her wild hair and funky attitude. It was hard to believe that next year this time, our lives would be so different. I wondered if we would still be a couple or if we'd choose opposite paths. That was the question that had burned in my mind all day.

On this day when everyone was giving thanks, I was thankful for Indigo. As I watched her do the Cupid Shuffle, I tried to imagine my life without her. I couldn't. She belonged there. Like the coffee table in our living room, it just belonged. And without it, the room wouldn't be complete.

She gave me a little smile and at that moment I knew that she would always be a part of me and I would be a part of her. I didn't know what our future held, but I knew that wherever I was in this huge world, Indigo Summer would be there, too.

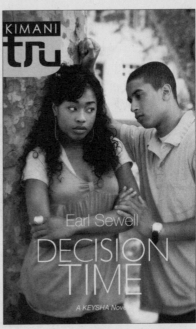

New school, new rules...

Going from high school to college is a big adjustment—but not if you're Kenya Posey. Even far from her Jersey turf, she's the one girls envy and boys want. And with her BFF Lark also on campus, could things get any better? If you're Lark, the answer is *yes.* Kenya's too self-absorbed to see beyond her fabulous new life. And when Kenya's brother Eric brings drama to her door, things are about to change....

Coming the first week of August 2009 wherever books are sold.

DIRTY SOUTH
A sequel to DIRTY JERSEY

Phillip Thomas Duck

www.KimaniTRU.com
www.myspace.com/kimani_tru

KPPTDI420809TR

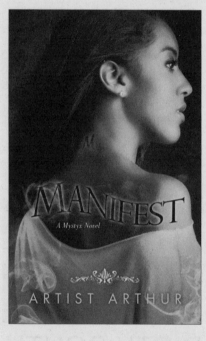